The One Great Gnome

FOR MY WIFE MARIA,

WHO HELPED ME MAKE LEMONADE

The
One Great
Gnome

WRITTEN BY JEFF DINARDO
WITH ILLUSTRATIONS BY JHON ORTIZ

ONE ELM
BOOKS

Egremont, Massachusetts

One Elm Books is an imprint of Red Chair Press LLC
www.redchairpress.com
www.oneelmpress.com
Free Discussion Guide available online

Publisher's Cataloging-In-Publication Data

Names: Dinardo, Jeffrey, author. | Ortiz, Jhon, illustrator.

Title: The One Great Gnome / written by Jeff Dinardo ; with illustrations by Jhon Ortiz.

Description: Egremont, Massachusetts : One Elm Books, [2020] | Interest age level: 008-012. | Summary: "May the moon and the stars always guide you safely. So says Vesper of Oglinoth to his new friend Sarah. Will she help him and the rest of the gnomes save their world from an unknown foe--and will Sarah find her own way back home?"--Provided by publisher.

Identifiers: ISBN 9781947159549 (paperback) | ISBN 9781947159594 (hardcover) | ISBN 9781947159556 (ebook)

Subjects: LCSH: Gnomes--Juvenile fiction. | Girls--Juvenile fiction. | Survival--Juvenile fiction. | Trolls--Juvenile fiction. | CYAC: Gnomes--Fiction. | Girls--Fiction. | Survival--Fiction. | Trolls--Fiction.

Classification: LCC PZ7.D6115 On 2020 (print) | LCC PZ7.D6115 (ebook) | DDC [Fic]--dc23

LC record available at https://lccn.loc.gov/2019949975

Main body text set in Basketville Regular 12/17

Printed in the United States of America

0920 2P CGF20

CHAPTER 1

This Isn't Manhattan

Sarah was having a dream, and it was a good one. She was walking arm in arm with her best friend Lily. They were on East 48th Street and looking in the window of Habington's Bookstore, one of their favorite hangouts. Lily loved books and reading as much as Sarah did. The girls hung out in the store so often that Mr. Habington hired them on weekends to help stock the new books. Sarah not only had the first pick of all the new titles, but she was getting paid for it too. Not bad for an eleven-year-old.

Then Sarah heard a noise. It sounded off in the distance somewhere.

Bang, bang—"OUCH!"

She woke from her dream and yawned. In those first moments, she was confused. She looked around through her squinting eyes. This wasn't her bedroom in the apartment building where she lived.

This room was different. It was big, bare, and filled with boxes.

Then she heard that thumping noise again.

Bang, bang, bang—"OUCH!"

That "OUCH" sounded like her father. Sarah stumbled out of bed.

"Dad, are you okay?" she called.

"I'm fine," called her father from the floor below. "Just whacked my thumb with the hammer… again! You should get up now," he added. "Breakfast is ready."

Sarah looked around. Now she remembered. She wasn't in Manhattan anymore, and this wasn't her room. Well, it was her room—her NEW room. Just the day before, she and her parents had packed up their cozy little apartment and moved here. And *here* was almost 100 miles away in Hadley, Connecticut. Her parents, despite her noisy and frequent protests, had bought this big, old, run-down farmhouse on five acres of land. Sarah's mom was a librarian and had just been hired to run the new Hadley Town Library. Her dad was a writer and had always wanted a separate room where he could work, rather than having to use the kitchen table in their tiny apartment. Her dad also had always thought of himself as a handyman and wanted this house because it needed a lot of work. Sarah and her mother both knew he was anything but "handy" when it came to fixing things. But her father loved to try anyway. So both of her parents were very happy about the move. Sarah had liked things just the way they were.

Sarah rubbed her eyes and stretched. She looked out the window. There was a thick layer of fog on the ground, but she could still make out the endless fields of trees and rolling hills. Not a single bookstore in view. No coffee shop on the corner, no flashing "Take Out" neon sign, no Chin's Fruit Market... nothing.

"Sarah," her dad called again. "If you don't move it, I'm gonna eat your breakfast."

Sarah turned from the window and went to get her slippers and robe. She looked around and saw nothing but boxes, so she just wrapped her comforter around her and walked down the steps. The wood creaked under her feet.

Sarah entered the kitchen. She saw her dad trying to hang some spices on a homemade rack. But nothing was straight, and the spices looked like they were about to slide off. Her father also seemed to be having a hard time because he had a towel wrapped around his thumb. He saw Sarah staring at it.

"I haven't found the bandages yet," he laughed. Sarah shook her head and smiled.

Last night, the kitchen had been nothing but piled-up furniture and boxes. But today, well, it looked like a kitchen. Her parents must have either stayed up late or gotten up early to get it into shape.

"About time." Her dad smiled as she sat down. Sarah ran her hands over the smooth, lime-green top. It was the same linoleum kitchen table with the mismatched chairs where she had always eaten. Even the old toaster—which seemed to only have one setting on it: BURNT—sat on the counter. It was nice to see.

Sarah felt something brush against her legs. "Smokey," she said, as she petted her cat. "I bet you like it here," she said. "Plenty of places to explore."

"She's been out all morning," said her father. He put a glass of orange juice and a bowl of cereal in front of Sarah. It was Chocolate Blasts, her favorite.

"Mom never lets me eat these," she said as she poured the milk over it. "Where is she anyway?"

"You know your mother," said Dad, as he sat down next to her. "She doesn't start her job at the library for another hour, but she was so excited, she went early." Sarah's dad grabbed one of the puffs of cereal from her bowl and popped it into his mouth.

"Hey, that's mine," Sarah laughed. "Get your own!" Her dad laughed, too, and got back to unpacking the last box in the kitchen.

"I know this isn't easy for you, kiddo," he said as he pulled out a jar of peanut butter and put it in a cupboard. "But this has been a dream of your mother's for a long time—to live in the country AND to be the head of a town library."

Sarah knew that. Even though they had lived in Manhattan, her mother had every issue of *Country Living* and tons of books on farmhouses and barns stacked on the overloaded shelves in the apartment.

"I know, I know," said Sarah as she ate. She wondered

what Lily was having for breakfast, but made herself think of something else.

"Can I explore what's around?" she asked her dad as she brought her empty cereal bowl to the sink.

"Well, I don't have to worry about you being run down by a taxi here," said her father. "Go ahead. I'll just be alone in here unpacking… all by myself."

Sarah ran upstairs and found her clothes (in the second box she opened). After getting dressed she came down the creaking steps again and went out the front door. The fog had lifted, and she could see the yard a bit more easily. Although her parents had wanted her to come while they were looking, Sarah didn't see the house until they moved in the day before. She had hoped that if she didn't go see the house, maybe the move wouldn't happen. That didn't work out.

Sarah hopped onto the gravel driveway and followed it to where it met the road. At the mailbox she looked left and saw nothing but trees, and the road twisted around a bend and out of sight. She looked right and saw a newer house across the street. Sarah wondered if a girl close to her age lived there.

Sarah turned around and got a good look at the outside of her own house. It was big, and it looked as though it had been around a long time. It reminded her of the farmhouses she had seen in her mother's books, but this one didn't look nearly as nice. It was three stories tall and seemed to have once been painted white, but the paint was all cracked and flaky. The few shutters she could see hung at strange angles. Sarah looked up at the roof—many of the shingles had fallen off. Her mother had told her the house needed work, but it had "good bones." Sarah wasn't so sure.

She ran around back. There was a long stone wall, and she jumped on top of it. Instantly, the rock she was on started to slide, and she barely got back to the ground without falling. She made a mental note not to do that again.

The yard seemed enormous to Sarah. When she lived in Manhattan and wanted to run around, Sarah's mother would take her and Lily to Central Park, which is a huge park right in the middle of the city. No need to do that here. This backyard was already like a park. She counted at least four giant trees that she thought she could climb. And one even had a big branch to hang a swing from. She would have to tell her dad about that one.

As Sarah continued to look around, she saw a smaller house attached to the side of the main house. Her dad had said it was called a bungalow and was used as a guest house or as a place for a caretaker to live. It was in just as bad shape as the main house.

Then Sarah noticed something at the far side of the yard. It looked like another house, but it was tiny and almost all covered up with ivy. It looked like the vines had tried to swallow it whole. Sarah went closer. The building was about eight feet wide and about ten feet long. One side was a wall of windows, which were mostly broken. Sarah guessed it was a potting shed. She had never seen one in person, but she had read about them in her mother's magazines. Farmers used them to store supplies and to grow plants in early spring when it was still too cold outside. There was a door on one end, and Sarah pulled at the handle. As the door opened, it groaned as if it had rusted in place, but Sarah opened it just enough so she could climb inside. She knew her mother wouldn't like her playing near the broken glass, so she was glad her mother had already gone to work.

Sarah looked around. No doubt about it. It was a potting shed. There were ceramic planters all over the floor, mostly broken; an old twisted shovel; and even what looked like some very old packages of seeds. Sarah picked up a silver stake with a handle on it. It reminded her of a tiny sword, and still looked sharp. It had two stars and a moon carved into its side. Maybe it was a weeding tool. She put it back on the ground. There was a rickety counter in one corner of the shed. It was mostly covered with dirt and some broken glass, but Sarah noticed something on top, half-buried in dirt. She gently lifted off some pieces of glass and brushed it clean. It was a small, oval-shaped picture frame, no bigger than the palm of her hand. She rubbed the front of it against her jeans and looked at it. It was a photograph of two people standing in front of a house. Sarah looked carefully and noticed that the house looked just like her house, except new. The man was dressed like a farmer with overalls and tall boots, and his face was covered with a big, bushy, black beard. But even through all that hair, Sarah could see he had a kind face. The woman next to him was probably his wife. She had her hair pulled back tightly and wore a simple dress with an apron. It reminded Sarah of one of her favorite books: *Little House on the Prairie*. Sarah turned the frame over and saw some handwriting on the back. It was written in cursive and was very loopy, like the way her grandmother wrote when she sent Sarah letters. It was hard to make out.

Sarah squinted like she did when she was trying to concentrate really hard.

"Otis Gregory Grimwald and Lavenia Sally Grimwald," she read. "You don't hear names like that every day." Sarah thought they must have been the people who built the farm. Her house had been their house, and this potting shed was probably where Lavenia started the plants from seeds. Sarah tucked the frame into the soft pocket of her sweatshirt. Her mom and dad would love to see this.

Sarah was just turning to leave when something caught her eye. It looked like a little gray shoe that was sticking out from under an overturned planter. Sarah carefully lifted the planter and laid it aside. The shoe was part of a statue. It looked like a little elf, or gnome, made out of stone. He was about three feet tall and dressed in a suit, and on his head was a pointed hat. Sarah had seen these in her mother's books. They were garden statues that people put in their yards for good luck.

"Why, hello there," said Sarah as she carefully stood him up. "You don't look too happy, do you?" she asked as she wiped the dust off of his face with her sleeve. She was right.

The statue was not smiling like the ones she had seen in the books. His face looked like he was worried or scared.

"I bet you just don't like being in this cold place," she said as she bent down and picked him up. He was a lot heavier than she expected. Sarah squeezed through the door with her prize and carried him back to the house. Her dad was now setting up the furniture in the living room.

"What do you have there?" he asked, wiping his sweaty brow with his sleeve. Sarah held up the statue for him to see.

"Ewww. Not a very happy looking fellow," he said, making a face to match the statue's. "Where did you find him?"

"He was in the old potting shed," said Sarah. " I'm going to put him in my room."

Sarah's father laughed. "Are you sure you want that in your room?" he said. "Maybe we can put him out in the front yard to scare away the wolves."

"Dad! There are no wolves in Connecticut!" snapped Sarah, although she wasn't too sure. She looked at his little face again. "I think he just needs a friend."

Sarah's dad smiled and rubbed the top of her head. "Sure, kiddo, go ahead."

CHAPTER 2

Vesper of Oglinoth

Sarah looked around her room to try to find a place for the statue. It was still just a sea of boxes. Sarah decided to lay the statue on her bed as she started to clean up. As she hung up her clothes and emptied her boxes, Sarah talked to her new friend. She told him about Lily, her old school, and how she wanted to be a writer like her father when she grew up.

When the last box was emptied and put out in the hallway, Sarah looked around. It looked just like her old room, but a lot bigger—and neater, too. Sarah knew it wouldn't stay like that for long.

She picked up the statue and placed him on her dresser by the mirror. "No, that's not right," she said. Then she picked him up again and put him by her nightstand.

"That looks better," she said. "I think you'll like it here." Sarah even turned him so he could face the window. Just then, she noticed something she had not seen before. On the side of the statue, there was a carved scabbard or sheath. Sarah recognized this from her book *The Three Musketeers*—it was where people kept daggers or swords.

"Maybe you're upset because you're missing your sword," she said. Then Sarah remembered the silver stake she had seen in the shed. "And I think I know where it is!" she added as she ran from the room. "I'll be right back!"

Sarah ran down the creaky stairs, two at a time, out the door and past her father, who was bringing the empty boxes to the street. "Whoa! What's the hurry?" was all her father could say as she sped past and was out to the shed in less than a minute.

She squeezed in through the shed door again and looked around. There, on the stone floor, she found the little sword. She picked it up and looked at it. She didn't know if her father would approve, so she put it in her sweatshirt pocket and walked calmly back to the front of the house and up to her room. When she got upstairs, she closed the door.

She looked at the little sword in her hand and at the sheath on the side of the statue. "Hmm, I think this IS yours," she said. Sarah gently slid the sword into place. It was a perfect fit.

Suddenly, the statue started to move. At first Sarah thought she was imagining it. The statue almost seemed to make a little hop, then another, like popcorn right before it bursts open. Sarah looked around her room to see if everything was jumping. *Maybe Connecticut has earthquakes*, she thought. But nothing else was moving. Sarah was going to run away, but she had to know what was happening. She jumped on her bed and hid under the covers, just letting her head stick out the tiniest bit. The statue jumped and jittered until it fell from the nightstand and landed on the floor with a thud.

Sarah couldn't see it now, but the shaking seemed to have stopped. At least she couldn't hear it anymore. Sarah slowly crept to the edge of her bed and peeked over the side. She came face to face with a little creature that was looking up at her.

"Ahhh!" Sarah screamed.

"Ahhhhhhh!" screamed the creature. It was the statue, and he was alive!

The little fellow jumped under her desk, but stuck his hand out and waved his sword in the air. "Stay away from me, troll!" he stammered.

"Troll!" said Sarah, feeling indignant. She hopped out of bed and stood up tall. "I am not a troll," she said in a booming voice. "I am a girl!"

The creature stayed where he was, but she could see his face peeking out at her. He looked like a frightened rabbit. Sarah felt bad for sounding so mean.

"I'm sorry," she said in her own voice. "I didn't mean to frighten you. Are you a gnome or an elf?"

"An elf?" boomed the creature. Now it was his turn to be angry. He wiggled out from under the desk and stood to his full height, which Sarah noticed was just below her waist.

"An elf?" he repeated. "Do I look eight feet tall with long pointed ears with hair growing out of them?" He stamped his little feet on the floor.

She couldn't help but laugh. "Well, I've never met an elf," she said, "…so I wouldn't know. But none of the ones I ever read about sounded like that!"

Even though the creature still held tightly to his little sword, Sarah knew he did not mean her any harm. She sat down beside him.

"What are you, then?" she asked.

The creature must have known that Sarah did not mean him any harm either, because he slid his sword into its sheath. He bowed gracefully while removing his hat.

"I am Vesper of Oglinoth," he said. "I am of the great race called gnomes. But you may just call me Vesper."

Sarah got a good look at him now. This gnome was dressed in clothes that were all shades of olive green, except his hat, which was rust in color, like leaves in the fall. He wore a vest with a jacket on top that hung low on his back. His shoes looked rough and built for hiking. His face was small, but he was no child. His long white beard hung down to his belt. He looked like a small relative of Santa Claus, but not fat at all—he was lean and in very good shape.

Sarah stuck out her hand and gently shook Vesper's. "I am Sarah Maria Arroyo," she said. "But just call me Sarah."

They both heard the screen door downstairs swing open and bang shut. Sarah thought her father must have come back inside. Vesper hid under the desk again.

"Is everything okay, Sarah?" her father called from the base of the steps. "I thought I heard shouting when I was outside."

Sarah smiled at Vesper, letting him know everything was fine. "It's okay," she called back. "It was just me playing with the elf... I mean, gnome!"

As her dad went back to his work, Vesper climbed out from his hiding place. He seemed to feel ashamed at being so skittish.

"I'm usually not so scared," he said as he brushed his beard with his hand. "But I've never been to the upper world before, and I didn't know what to expect."

"Upper world?" questioned Sarah. "This isn't the upper world. We call this place Hadley, Connecticut."

"I have heard that name before." Vesper said. "I think it

was in a story the Ogg told us." He rubbed his eyes. "But I don't remember. Everything is very foggy now."

Sarah was about to pull a chair out for him, but thought it would be too tall. So she stayed on the floor next to him. "Well, you've been a statue for who knows how long!" she said. "It must take a while to feel better."

Sarah jumped up. "I bet you're hungry," she said. "Let me get you something!"

Vesper looked relieved. "Yes, maybe just a piece of Flemite or a tankard of Breem, if you have them?"

Sarah just smiled and ran downstairs. She didn't know what he was talking about, so she figured she would just bring him back a bunch of different things and see what he liked. She grabbed a plate and filled it with pieces of cheese, some oatmeal bread, Oreos, some raw broccoli, a box of raisins, some Jell-O pudding, and a tall glass of orange juice. Just as she turned into the hallway, her father came into the room.

"What's all this?" he said as he saw Sarah's overflowing arms.

"Umm, just hungry!" she called as she ran past him and started up the stairs. But she stopped halfway and turned around. "Dad. Do we have any Breem?"

"Do we have any what?" her father called back, still astonished at his little girl's sudden appetite.

"Never mind!" she called as she raced up the stairs, ran into her room, and shut the door.

CHAPTER 3

A Time to Remember

Vesper proved to have a good appetite and was very open to trying new foods. He didn't care for the oatmeal bread (too spongy), and he wouldn't even touch the Jell-O ("gnomes never eat food that jiggles," he said). But the broccoli and raisins were his favorites, and he wanted to know if Sarah had the recipe for Oreos (she didn't, but she brought him another handful).

When Vesper finished eating, Sarah decided to ask him some questions. She didn't know where to begin.

"Where are you from?" seemed the logical starting place.

"I said, I am from Oglinoth," Vesper said, as if the answer was obvious.

"Yes, yes," said Sarah. "But where is Oglinoth?"

"Ah, I understand," said Vesper as he took a sip of the orange juice (nice, but a bit too sour for gnomes). Vesper wiped his mouth with the tip of his beard and arranged himself more comfortably on the floor. Sarah did the same.

"My head's a bit foggy still," said Vesper, "but some things are very clear. I was born in Oglinoth, which is the biggest village in Oberith, the country of gnomes. My father and mother are trackers, and I want to be one too."

"What's a tracker?" said Sarah, who suddenly wished she had started writing this all down.

Vesper stroked his long beard. "Trackers track," he said. "They track game in the woods for food. They track the paths through the thick forests to get to neighboring villages. They track the stars in the sky to tell when it's planting season. They track anything that needs to be tracked. But the things they track best are trolls."

Sarah remembered he had called her a troll when he first came alive again.

"Do trolls look like humans... like me?" she asked.

Vesper coughed and cleared his throat. "Umm, sorry about that. No, no, trolls definitely do not look like upper-worlders. They are foul beasts. Our mortal enemies!"

Sarah could see Vesper's face changing. It was clear he did not like trolls.

"They are bigger than gnomes, about as tall as your kind. They are all covered in thick, coarse hair. And the worst part of them is their smell. It's enough to turn your stomach for a week."

"Why don't they take baths?" Sarah asked.

"HA!" laughed Vesper. "A troll wouldn't know what a bath was. They can't even communicate. They have the brains of a rock. They live by themselves and are very lazy. They hide in the forests and steal our chickens, our pigs, and the fruit from our trees. There's not a kind bone in their bodies, and if I had my way, there would be none left!" And with that,

Vesper stood up, pulled his sword from his scabbard, and pointed it at the sky.

Sarah thought she had better change the subject.

"Calm down, Vesper," she said. "How did you get here? And, why were you a statue?"

Vesper put his sword away and sat back down.

"Why I am here, I do not remember," he said. "I think there was something that I had to do?" Vesper stared out of the window, as if his memory could be found in the maple tree outside.

"And becoming a statue is easy for a gnome... but it's embarrassing," he said. He pointed to his sword.

"A gnome's sword is his most precious companion. It is given to us at birth, and we are to keep it with us always. If we ever lose that sword, we turn to stone until it is returned to our hands or our scabbards."

"So you lost yours, and that's why I found you as a statue!" Sarah said. "What happened?"

Vesper scratched his chin. "It was so long ago.... Yes, yes, I remember!" he said. "A beast. A terrible beast attacked me! I had just gotten through to the upper world when a huge, hairy beast jumped me. It had large fangs and sharp claws, and when I went to grab my sword, it attacked me and knocked it from my hand! And that's when I turned to stone."

Sarah tried to imagine what kind of awful beasts they had here in Connecticut. She'd certainly never heard about them in Manhattan!

Just then, Sarah's cat Smokey padded into the room.
He jumped up on Sarah's bed. She reached out to pet him.

"BEAST!" yelled Vesper, drawing his sword again. "That
is the same kind of beast that attacked me! Get away, Sarah,
and I shall run it through!"

He lunged at the cat, but Smokey hissed and, with one
paw, scratched him right on his round nose.

"Ouch!" yelled Vesper as he grabbed his nose. "Ouch,
ouch, ouch!" He jumped around the room so much
Sarah had to grab him and set him on her bed to calm
him down. Smokey calmly hopped off and walked out of
the room.

Sarah looked at Vesper's nose. It was just a little scratch. "That is a cat!" she said. "A cute fluffy kitty! And what's more, he's my fluffy kitty, so there will be no *running it through* today!"

Vesper felt ashamed. "Well, the one that attacked me must have been a lot bigger… and meaner, maybe." Vesper hung his head low. "It's no use," he said. "I'm not a tracker or a great hunter. I'm actually a cook. I was never good enough to become a tracker like my parents. I use my sword to cut bread more than anything."

Sarah felt bad for Vesper. "Do you know how long you were turned to stone?" she asked, trying to change the subject.

"I don't know," said Vesper. "But I think it was a long time. I remember that even though I was stone and couldn't move, I could still hear and sense things around me. I remember times when I was very hot, and other times I was very cold, and sometimes even covered with a blanket of cold for months at a time."

"Snow," said Sarah. "Go on."

"I just remember the periods of hot and cold came several times before I woke up here in this place."

"So you must have been stone for many years," said Sarah. "I wonder if your family was worried."

With that, Vesper jumped up as if a firecracker had gone off in his shoe. "I remember! I remember!" he said grabbing Sarah by the sleeve.

"Remember what?" Sarah cried.

"I remember why I came to the upper world!" he stammered as he hopped off the bed. "My family is in trouble and I was sent on a mission to get help!"

It was all Sarah could do to keep up with Vesper. He jumped to his feet, then down the stairs, and tried to figure out how to reach the handle on the front door.

"Stop—wait for me!" she protested. She was afraid Vesper might try to slice open the door with his sword if she didn't let him out. She grabbed the handle, turned it, and opened the door. Vesper ran as fast as his little legs could carry him. He looked around, then went straight for the backyard.

Sarah's father came up the stairs from the basement. He held a lamp in his hand. "Stop what?" he asked. "I wasn't going anywhere."

Sarah turned and faced her father. She didn't have time to explain all about Vesper, and his coming to life, right then and there. "I know, Dad," she said quickly. "It was just me playing again! I'm going to play outside for a while!" And with that, she ran outside to try and catch up to Vesper before he disappeared.

Her father called out from the front porch. "In a few minutes we're going to stop by the library so we can bring Mom her lunch, so don't go far."

"I'll be right back!" yelled Sarah, as she disappeared around the corner of the house where she had seen Vesper go.

Sarah couldn't have known that she would not be back for a very long time.

CHAPTER 4

The Passage Home

As Sarah got to the backyard, she quickly looked around. Where had the gnome gone? She ran by the stone wall, but didn't see anything. She looked in the windows of the bungalow. Nothing there but empty rooms. She even looked up into the large trees in the yard. No Vesper. Beyond her yard was what seemed like an endless forest. Vesper could be long gone by now.

Then she heard a crash, as if a dish or pot had just broken. Sarah turned to look at the potting shed and ran right for it.

Sarah saw that the door had already been pulled open, and she squeezed herself in. At first, everything was silent, and Sarah thought she must have gone to the wrong place. Then, suddenly, a clay pot flew through the air and crashed at her feet. Someone was in the corner of the potting shed, trying to move the debris of broken pots and glass out of the way.

"I know it's here," she heard a familiar and determined voice say. Sarah dodged another pot as she pulled back a bench to get a better view. There she saw Vesper in the corner pushing the last pot aside. He looked up at Sarah and smiled.

"I knew it was here!" Vesper said. He clapped the dust

from his hands and pointed down at the ground. Sarah knelt beside him. There on the ground was what looked like a trapdoor. Sarah brushed away a layer of dirt with her hand. It was indeed a door. It was small and square, with an arch along the top. Sarah could see it was beautifully carved, with a leaf border design outlining its shape. It had two large metal hinges that were shaped like the heads of dragons. There was no handle or knob on the door, but it did have a small keyhole in its center.

"What is it?" asked Sarah.

"It's an entrance to my world," said Vesper. "It's called a gnome-way."

"Do you have the key?" she asked Vesper as she outlined the shape of the keyhole with her finger.

"Key? Key?" said Vesper as he felt in his vest pockets. "Where is the key?" He started pulling over pots and moving shovels. Sarah started to look too.

"Tell me… what happened?" she asked as she looked up on the top shelves. "What happened to your family?"

Vesper kept on pulling things apart, searching while he answered her. "The trolls!" he said. "The trolls were taking over the countryside! They were marching on the village, and the Ogg sent me to try and get help before it was too late." Then Vesper stopped searching and looked right into Sarah's face. "The day before I left, they had captured my parents!"

Sarah stopped searching and put her hand on Vesper's shoulder. "That's awful!" she said. She understood why Vesper hated trolls so much. They kept looking for the key.

"Why come to Connecticut—I mean, the upper world?" said Sarah. "What would you find here?"

Vesper stopped searching and looked forlornly at Sarah.

"I didn't know where to go or who could help us," he said, "but I always remembered the great stories of this world that the Ogg told us, and I thought maybe I could find someone to help."

"Who is the Ogg?" said Sarah. She had heard Vesper mention that name a few times.

"The Ogg?" said Vesper astoundingly. "The One Great Gnome, of course! He is the leader of all the gnomes. He is a very important man," added Vesper proudly. "And I was his personal cook!"

"I am sure he is very dear to your heart," said Sarah.

"Heart!" said Vesper with a laugh. He quickly opened his vest and undid two buttons on his shirt. There, hanging on a chain in front of his heart, was a metal key.

Vesper took the chain off and placed the key in the lock. It turned with a sharp "click" sound. Together they opened the small door, which proved to be quite heavy. Sarah peeked in. All she could see was a black hole going straight down into nothingness. There was a pungent smell of dirt and earth.

Vesper grabbed Sarah's hand. "I need to see if I'm too late!"

Vesper bowed low to Sarah and gently kissed the back of her hand. "May the moon and the stars always guide you safely," he said. And with that, Vesper jumped into the hole and disappeared.

"Wait!" said Sarah. But it was too late. The hole seemed to have swallowed Vesper up.

Sarah felt awful. She had just met her first new friend, and now he was gone. "There must be something I can do to help!"

Then, without even thinking, Sarah jumped into the hole herself and disappeared.

CHAPTER 5

A Whole New World

Sarah was terrified. She was falling, tumbling in the air, faster and faster. She kept expecting to hit the ground at any moment. She was too terrified to scream. She tried to look below her, but the darkness was so complete that Sarah couldn't even see her own hand. She was surprised by how long and how far she kept falling. She didn't want to hit the bottom, but she kept wondering when it was going to end.

Then, to her surprise, her body started to slow. In a moment, she felt herself floating as if she were underwater. Then she saw a door open in front of her, and she slid through it and landed with a soft thud on the ground. Sarah saw it was a similar-looking doorway to the one she jumped into, but this one was mounted to the side of a tree. Sarah stood up. It felt good to be on the ground again. She looked around. It was very dark, but her eyes slowly got accustomed to it. Sarah looked up. She was surprised to see a clear night sky filled with stars.

"Stars!" said Sarah. She rubbed her eyes on her sleeve. "How can there be a sky or stars underground? And it was still morning at home!" The stars she saw in this sky did not match any constellations she knew about. But astronomy was not her best subject. Her mother and father both enjoyed looking at the stars, and sometimes took Sarah to the roof of their apartment building in Manhattan to see them if the night was clear. Her parents! Sarah hadn't thought about what she was doing when she jumped in that hole after Vesper. Her father would be looking for her soon. He was bound to look in the potting shed. What would he do when he saw the open doorway?

"My best bet is to find Vesper," Sarah muttered to herself. "But where did he go?"

Sarah looked around. She seemed to be at the edge of a forest. She heard crickets chirping and felt a breeze blowing. She saw a light in the distance, so, not having a better idea, she started walking in that direction.

As she got closer, she noticed the light was coming from a window in a small hut on the end of a field. It looked like it was made from dirt or sod, with a thatched roof. Sarah thought it reminded her of houses she saw in her fairy tale books. She half expected to meet Little Red Riding Hood at the door. As Sarah got closer to the hut, she could smell the sweet scent of flowers. She inhaled deeply. "Wonderful," she said.

She reached the hut. She had to bend down to knock on the door. She noticed it looked very similar to the trapdoor in the potting shed, but this one had plain, simple hinges and no carving on it. Sarah knocked again, but no one answered. Sarah walked by the window and peeked in. She saw a simple room with a lamp hanging from the ceiling and a small wooden table and chairs.

"Got ya, beastie!" bellowed a voice from behind Sarah. She felt something sharp poking her in the rear end.

"I… I don't mean any harm," said Sarah, without turning around. "I'm just trying to find my friend."

"Friends!" said the voice. "Since when do trolls have friends?"

That was the second time someone had called Sarah a troll that day.

"I am not a troll!" yelled Sarah, and she was so mad she turned around quickly. The creature behind her was surprised and jumped back a little. Sarah saw what looked like a gnome, but this one was female and looked much older than Vesper. She had the same type of clothes Vesper had, but they were torn and ragged, and an old apron was tied around her waist. She wore no pointed hat on her head. Rather, she had an old kerchief tied around it. She held a cane in her hands, with the end pointing at Sarah. She looked more scared than Sarah did.

"I'm sorry," said Sarah, more gently now. "I'm just lost!"

The gnome looked a bit relieved. "I see you are no friend of a troll," she said as she lowered her cane. "Quickly, then, quickly—inside you go!" The gnome beckoned for Sarah to join her in the house.

When the old gnome gestured for her to take a seat, Sarah thought she might break it if she tried so she just stood where she was. The gnome quickly shut the door and bolted it tightly, then she slid a chair next to Sarah.

"Can't be too careful these days!" she said. "Nasty creatures all about! But they don't bother Mazy!" The gnome laughed, and Sarah could see she only had one tooth in her open mouth.

"Let's get a proper look at you," the gnome said, as she stood on the chair and removed the lamp from its hook on the ceiling. Sarah noticed that the lamp did not have a flame in it. The light was coming from a tiny creature that stood inside the lamp. It had silvery wings like a butterfly, but its body looked like a tiny person. The glow seemed to come from its whole body. It saw Sarah looking at it and it smiled and waved. It seemed quite happy where it was.

"Not enough light," said Mazy. She turned her head, put two fingers into her mouth, and blew a loud piercing whistle. In a few seconds, another shining butterfly creature came through the window, flew right into the lamp, and hugged the first creature. The glow from the lamp was now much brighter.

"Much better," said Mazy. She held the lamp close to Sarah's face. "Too tall for a gnome," she muttered as she looked her over. "Not hairy enough for a troll." She held a lock of Sarah's hair and sniffed it. "Smells too good, too," she laughed. "Not tall or ugly enough for an elf! Well, you seem friendly, but what kind of beastie are you?"

"I'm a person!" said Sarah. "A girl."

The gnome seemed surprised. "A girl? A human girl?!" She laughed and slapped her hand on her side. "Mazy's never seen a human girl before. Thought they were only in fairy tales."

Now Sarah laughed. "Until a few hours ago," she said, "I never thought gnomes really existed. My name is Sarah."

"I'm Mazy," said the old gnome. "'Crazy Mazy,' some call me."

"Oh, that's awful!" said Sarah. "I'm sure they don't mean it."

"Of course they mean it!" said Mazy. "And I *am* crazy. But I'm smarter than they think!"

Mazy hopped off the chair, then went to a cupboard and pulled out two wooden cups. She took a bottle off the shelf and pulled the cork out with her lone tooth. She poured some purple liquid into each cup and placed one on the table near Sarah.

Sarah looked at the liquid and smelled it. It smelled like the peppermint tea her mother always drank.

"Go on, drink it," said Mazy. "It'll grow hair on your chin!"

"What?" said Sarah. "I'm not sure…"

Mazy laughed. "Just an expression, girl!" With that, Mazy drank her cupful in one big gulp. Sarah looked at her own cup and took a little sip. It was sweet and warm. She took a bigger drink. Mazy had set the lamp on the table; inside it, the two butterfly creatures seemed to be having their own pleasant conversation.

"Now tell Mazy why you were snooping outside," said the old gnome.

Sarah set her cup down. "I was trying to figure out where my friend Vesper went, so I…"

"Vesper!" said Mazy. "Vesper, the Ogg's cook?"

"Yes, that's him," said Sarah. "Do you know him?"

Mazy rubbed her chin and looked out the window.

"We all thought Vesper was dead," she said. "He left so long ago… I think about five years now., just as all the trouble really began."

"Was it the trolls?" asked Sarah.

Mazy looked right into her eyes.

"It was the trolls, all right!" she said. "They've taken over, and they've captured all the gnomes. All except me!"

CHAPTER 6

Into the Woods

Mazy told Sarah all she knew about the trolls and what had happened. Sarah just had to find Vesper and tell him.

"Do you know where Vesper would go?" she asked Mazy.

Mazy picked up the cups and put them away. "Hard to say," said Mazy. "Probably went to his parents' home. That's not too far away."

"I have to go!" said Sarah.

"Tomorrow morning," said Mazy.

"No, I have to go now," said Sarah. "I have to warn Vesper before something happens to him!"

"Something will happen to you if you go out this time of night!" said Mazy. "The dark is when the trolls come out. They hate light. Drives them mad. But come nightfall, they crawl around like bugs."

Mazy saw the determined look on Sarah's face.

"Very well," the woman sighed. She gestured for Sarah to join her at the window and pointed at something off in the distance. "See that bright star in the sky—the big one over there?"

"I see it," said Sarah.

"You head that way, and keep that star always on your left. In about three miles, you'll run right into their house or what's left of it."

"What do you mean?" said Sarah.

"No one's been taking care of that place since Vesper's parents were captured and Vesper disappeared," Mazy said. "It's all run down now."

Sarah thanked Mazy as the old gnome unlatched the door. "Wait a second," said Mazy, lifting the edge of her apron and pulling out a small sword. It looked a lot like Vesper's, but much smaller.

"I can't take that," said Sarah.

"Not giving it to you," Mazy laughed. "I don't want to end up some statue in a troll's garden." Mazy peeked outside, then shuffled to a garden that grew alongside the hut. Sarah noticed small yellow flowers that grew all around. With her sword, Mazy cut a handful and handed them to Sarah. Sarah inhaled. That was the same sweet aroma she had smelled when she walked across the field.

"They're called Dragon's Breath," said Mazy.

"They are beautiful," said Sarah.

"They're better than that!" said Mazy. "They're my secret!"

"Secret?" asked Sarah.

"My secret to stopping trolls!" said Mazy. "Why do you think I never got captured?"

"Because of flowers?" said Sarah reluctantly.

"Because of their smell!" said Mazy, and she laughed and danced a little jig. "Trolls hate their sweet smell. Won't come anywhere near them. I spent years planting a whole field of them!"

"Did you tell the other gnomes?" Sarah asked.

"Tried," said Mazy. "No one listened. No one listens to Crazy Mazy!"

Sarah kissed Mazy on the head. Then she tried to remember what Vesper had said.

"May the moon and the stars always guide you safely," she said.

Mazy smiled. "You'd make a good gnome."

Sarah took off in the direction Mazy had told her to go. She held the Dragon's Breath out in front of her and marched out into the night.

Sarah walked quickly and tried not to think about the danger. She looked all around her at the landscape she was passing. Although it was dark, she could easily make out the rolling hills in the distance. She saw many dwellings that looked like Mazy's, all scattered about. But none of them had any lights on.

Sarah came to a thick forest of trees. It was very dense and hard to see into. Sarah took a deep breath, then plunged on in. She decided to run. She wanted to get to the other side as quickly as she could. After a few minutes she stopped. Sarah tried to look up to the sky to see if she could see the star. But when she looked up, all she could see was the thick branches and leaves. Sarah felt a little nervous, but she guessed at the direction and started running again.

Then Sarah heard a sound like something was running nearby. She stopped and listened. The sound stopped just after she did. But there was a smell. A smell so bad Sarah held her nose for a second. Sarah waved the Dragon's Breath all around and started running again. The footsteps came back, and more of them joined in. Sarah heard creatures running behind trees and even jumping in the branches above her head. Sarah ran faster.

Her foot got caught on a tree root and she fell to the ground. Her flowers scattered all around her. Sarah didn't stop to pick them up. She jumped to her feet and ran on. She could see the end of the forest up ahead. She was just about through.

Then something jumped out of a tree ahead of her, blocking the way. It was so dark that is was hard to see it clearly but she could see its yellow eyes, which seemed to glow in the dark. It was taller than Vesper, and much wider, with long, dangling arms at its sides. The air was filled with its awful stench. Sarah knew it was a troll. Another one landed behind her, blocking that way. Two more landed, one to each side of her. She was trapped. Sarah looked around. She grabbed a branch on the ground, picked it up, and waved it as she spun around.

"Stay away from me," she yelled, "or I'll knock you to Brooklyn!"

The creature in front edged closer. It came near enough for Sarah to see it clearly now. It was all covered in thick fur. Its face was barely visible, but those eyes still glowed. It had a snout that made it look like a cross between a wolf and a man. It opened its mouth and Sarah saw its row of yellow, crooked teeth.

Sarah raised her branch and got ready to strike.

"YAAAAAAAA!" came a shout from the edge of the forest. The trolls turned to look. So did Sarah. The moonlight reflected off of a shiny blade—a figure carrying a sword was running their way.

"Get away from her, you beasts!" yelled Vesper, as he waved his sword at them all.

Sarah smiled. "Yeah, beat it!" she added, waving her stick.

The trolls ran off into the deep forest and were soon gone.

"Vesper!" said Sarah. "I've been trying to find you!" She gave him a hug.

"I heard someone yelling," said Vesper, who seemed out of breath. "I never thought it would be you. Why did you follow me through the gnome-way?"

Sarah looked at Vesper. "We're friends," she said, "and friends help each other. You were pretty brave just now. Like a tracker."

Vesper smiled. "Maybe, but I was terrified! Come on— let's get to my parents' house before those trolls come back," he added. "It's pretty run-down, but I think we'll be safe."

CHAPTER 7

By the Fire

In a few minutes they came to the house. It was much bigger than Mazy's and was made out of stone, but it also had a thatched roof. It looked like it had seen better days. The roof was caving in some places, and there were holes right through areas of the stone walls. There seemed to be the remains of a garden in the front yard, but it was choked with nothing but weeds. It looked like no one had been there for a long time.

When they entered, a warm fire crackling in the fireplace greeted them.

Vesper looked around forlornly. "The last time I was here, the house was beautiful," he said. "Now it's just a run-down shack."

Sarah thought she should change the subject. "You got a nice fire going," she said. "And what smells so good?"

Vesper brightened up at the mention of this. "It's not much, but it's a stew I often made for the Ogg. I had to use the ingredients I could find. I was just seasoning it when I heard you yelling in the forest."

"I'm glad you heard!" said Sarah. She didn't like to think

about what might have happened if he hadn't. "I may have stopped one or two of them," she said as she warmed her hands at the fire, "but I don't think I could have taken them all on!"

Vesper laughed. "You'd make a good gnome!" he said.

"That's just what Mazy said," Sarah added.

"Crazy Mazy?" said Vesper. "I would stay away from her."

"I don't think she's crazy," said Sarah. "She's very nice, and she even told me how to keep trolls away."

"Didn't seem to work very well," he said.

Sarah was mad. "Without Mazy, I wouldn't know what happened while you were gone!"

Vesper arranged a table with the only two spoons and bowls he found that weren't broken. He poured out some stew for each of them. He pulled up two old chairs, but saw that Sarah was much too large to sit in either of them. Vesper looked around. "I have just the thing," he said, "if it's still here." He ran into one of the other rooms of the house, and came back carrying what appeared to be a full-size chair. Sarah helped him place it by the table. It wasn't a simple chair, like the one Vesper had; it seemed made to fit a full-sized person, and the armrests were carved into the paws of a dragon. The seat was covered in soft red velvet.

"Some chair!" said Sarah as she sat in it. It was very comfortable.

"That's a chair my father built for the Ogg," said Vesper as he proudly examined the fine carvings. "When he wasn't tracking, my father was a woodworker. He made this chair so when the Ogg visited, he had somewhere special to sit."

Sarah felt honored. "Is the Ogg large?" she asked. "I mean, for a gnome?"

"Yes," said Vesper. "He is, after all, the One Great Gnome. He's great in his kindness, his wisdom, and his size."

Sarah tasted the stew. "Wow, this is terrific!" she said.

Vesper smiled. "If I had all my spices here, it would really be something!"

After they had eaten, Sarah stood by the fire.

"You start," she said. "Tell me what happened before you left, and I will tell you what happened after."

Vesper poked the embers of the fire with a long stick. "Oglinoth was a beautiful place," he began. "We all lived in cozy homes, had plenty of food and never had any real worries. But I heard stories that it wasn't always like that."

"What do you mean?" asked Sarah.

"When my father's father was young, things were different," he said. "Gnomes lived in small caves in the hills, didn't know about books or music, and never helped each other. We were no better than the trolls!"

"What changed?" asked Sarah.

"Ahh," said Vesper with a smile. "That's when the One Great Gnome came. He alone brought us together, taught us to be a community. He helped the race of gnomes become what we are."

"He must be very old," said Sarah.

"Yes, very old," said Vesper, "and he doesn't get around like he used to. That's why I went to work for him as a cook, so he wouldn't have to worry about making his meals. There were several of us who had the honor of working for him."

"But what about the trolls?" asked Sarah.

"Well, there have always been trolls," said Vesper. "But they were nothing more than pests, really. They would come to try and steal a chicken or two, but even the smallest gnome could chase them away with a wave of his sword. Trolls never seemed to work together, so they lived their lives alone, poaching what they could from us. But then something happened. The trolls started working together, and as a group, they were much tougher than when they were alone. They started raiding homes—not just stealing chickens, but taking everything... sometimes even gnomes."

"And that's what happened to your parents?" asked Sarah sadly.

Vesper got up and added another log to the fire.

"I had been living at Mount Gnome," he said as he again took his seat. "That's where we built a home for the Ogg."

"A mountain?" asked Sarah. "Mazy told me about a mountain today."

"The Ogg didn't want a palace, even though we would gladly have built one for him," Vesper continued. "So we built a wonderful home for the Ogg at Mount Gnome. But he didn't want to live in a mountain all alone, so he helped us build libraries, concert halls, and museums. All in the mountain! It's a place that's always busy with gnomes and events. The Ogg loved it there!"

"Why did he send you for help?" asked Sarah. She

really wished she had remembered to bring paper to write all this down.

"The countryside was overrun by trolls," said Vesper. "Everyone came to the mountain for safety. The trackers, including my parents, were sent out to try and find out what had happened, but we never heard from them again… except for one lone tracker. She made it back and said the trolls were headed right for the mountain. That's when the Ogg sent me to try and find help." Vesper's face tightened. "A lot of good I did."

"It's okay," said Sarah. "You are here now, and I'll help!"

Vesper smiled faintly. "What did Crazy… I mean, what did Mazy tell you?"

"It's not good," said Sarah, and she began to tell Vesper Mazy's story. "All the gnomes except her have been carted away. She said she overheard some trolls talking once, and they said…"

"Trolls don't talk," said Vesper. "A grunt or growl, maybe, but they can't…"

"Do you want to hear what she said or not?" said Sarah.

"Sorry, go on," said Vesper.

"She said that she overheard some trolls talking, and it seems like all the gnomes are being held captive in the mountain! She also said that the trolls were getting their orders from someone they called Krep, or Krunk, or something like that."

"Well, I'm not sure what to believe," said Vesper. "But it seems like we need to get to the mountain and see if it's true."

Sarah stood up. "I'm ready!" she said.

"Not tonight," said Vesper. "Too many trolls out at night. We'll go in the morning, when all the trolls are hiding."

"Mazy said they hated the light," said Sarah.

"That she was right about," said Vesper. "I hope she's not right about the rest."

Vesper and Sarah did the best they could to board up the door and the windows, so no trolls could get in.

"Do you have any Dragon's Breath?" asked Sarah.

"Why? Do you want tea?" asked Vesper.

"No," said Sarah. "Mazy said trolls couldn't stand the smell of Dragon's Breath."

Vesper just made a face. "I never heard that," he said. "I think my mother used to grow it in her garden, but that's all just weeds now." Vesper threw several other logs onto the fire to keep the room bright. "They won't want to come anywhere near this!" he said.

Vesper made up two beds by the fire, and he and Sarah got into them. Sarah's feet hung out the back, but if she scrunched up, she was fine. They both lay still, trying to sleep. Sarah had a hard time falling asleep. So much had happened to her today. She wondered what her parents were doing. She tried not to think about it.

"Vesper," she whispered, "I think I'm kind of afraid of what we will find."

"Me too," said Vesper. "I'm glad we're doing it together."

And with that, they both fell silent, and as the fire warmed the room, they both drifted off into an uneasy sleep.

CHAPTER 8

A Journey Begins

Sarah woke up groggy the next day. She looked around the room. The fire was still burning brightly, and Vesper was already up. She heard the sounds of pots and pans from the next room. She had a funny thought. Two mornings ago Sarah had woken up in her familiar room in Manhattan. Yesterday morning she woke up in her new room in Hadley, Connecticut. This morning she was in a hut in the center of a gnome world. She wondered where she would wake up tomorrow.

"Ah, you're finally up," said Vesper from the doorway. "Breakfast is ready." Sarah stood up and stretched. Her body ached a bit from being scrunched up all night. She came into what appeared to be a kitchen. A wonderful smell greeted her.

"It's just eggs," said Vesper. "I found a few stray hens who were still roosting in the barn."

"It smells great," said Sarah with a yawn. "When did you get up?"

"With the first rays of the sun," said Vesper as he spooned equal amounts onto two plates. "It's when all gnomes get up."

Sarah yawned again and Vesper laughed. "I was getting worried," said Vesper, "that you would sleep all day."

"I always have a hard time waking up," said Sarah. "But I'm up now."

After breakfast, Vesper brought out two rough backpacks that were bulging at the seams.

"Provisions," he said. "It's a good day and a half to Mount Gnome, and I'm worried that we may not find any help along the way."

Sarah picked one up. It was heavy. "What's in it?' she asked as she struggled to put it on over her shoulder.

"Blankets, extra clothes," said Vesper, "some food I traded for with Mazy…"

"Mazy?" said Sarah. "You went to see Mazy?"

"Yes," said Vesper as he easily swung his own pack onto his back. "She was glad to hear you got here safely. Oh—she made me bring you this." Vesper reached over by the door and pulled out a bouquet of flowers.

"Dragon's Breath," laughed Sarah. She tucked the flowers into a side flap on her pack.

As they walked out the door, Vesper looked around at his parents' house. "I hope the next time I come back, it will be with my parents!" he said.

"I know it will be," said Sarah.

It was a beautiful day. Even though Sarah had been able to see some of her surroundings last night, it didn't compare to what she saw now. They were in a valley, and beautiful green hills ran up beside them. There were waving fields of grass and trees that Sarah had never seen before. They stopped and called into every hut or house they came to, but there was no response. No one was around, and some of the homes were in worse shape than Vesper's.

Sarah showed great interest in her new surroundings, and Vesper paused every now and again to point out a unique tree or plant to Sarah, like a bush with little purple berries that could cure aches and pains.

In one field, Vesper stopped short and pointed something out that was barely visible on the ground. It seemed to be made of metal, with sharp jaws on it.

"That's a troll trap," said Vesper. "I would never use one, but farmers have set them out for years."

"Looks nasty," said Sarah. "What do we do?"

Vesper looked around and grabbed a large branch that was lying on the ground. He stuck one end right into the trap.

SNAP! went the trap. The branch was cut in half.

"I'm no fan of trolls," said Vesper. "But I don't like these things."

At noon, they paused for lunch at the side of a fast-moving stream. The remains of a bridge stood at its bank. Vesper looked sadly at the splintered wood.

"This was once a beautiful place," he said. "It was one of the first projects the Ogg got us to build. It showed us we could work together as a community."

"It can be rebuilt," said Sarah.

Vesper found a shady spot under a tree and laid out their lunch. As they ate, Sarah noticed something flutter down from one of the branches—one of those creatures Sarah had seen in Mazy's lamp. It landed on the grass between Vesper and Sarah. Vesper barely even noticed it.

"Hello there," said Sarah as she looked at the creature. She held out her hand, and it climbed onto her palm. Slowly, Sarah brought her hand to her face so she could have a closer look. This creature looked slightly different from the ones she had seen last night. It had glistening silver wings.

"Sprite," said Vesper in between bites of his lunch.

"What did you say?" said Sarah as she continued to gaze at the little person with wings in her hand. The creature smiled and kept waving at her.

"It's called a sprite," said Vesper. "They're everywhere, and they glow at night. Gnomes use them as lights."

Sarah laughed. "A sprite light," she said. "Don't they mind being kept in those lamps?"

"Not at all," said Vesper. "We just whistle when we need

them, and the nearest one flutters over from the trees. When we don't need the light any more, they just fly away."

Sarah looked even closer at the one on her hand "Do you have a name?"

The sprite just went on smiling and waving.

"I've never known one who could talk," said Vesper. "And I still don't think trolls can talk, either."

Sarah smiled at Vesper. "I think I'll call her Frieda, after my little cousin."

The sprite fluttered off her hand and did a somersault in the air.

"I think she likes the name," said Vesper.

They gathered up their packs again and started off. Sarah waved goodbye to Frieda as the sprite fluttered back up to the tree. "We are making good time," said Vesper. "But I want us to get to the Statue of Liberty before nightfall."

"What?" said Sarah. "The Statue of Liberty—here?"

Vesper looked surprised. "You've heard of it?" he asked. "It's one of our oldest places. It sits on the northern border of Oglinoth. I think my father told me the Ogg built it mostly by himself long ago."

"This Ogg sounds more and more interesting," said Sarah. "I can't wait to meet him."

CHAPTER 9

Friend or Foe

Vesper and Sarah hiked all that afternoon. They traveled through many villages and past many houses. All of them were empty, and many were ransacked.

As the sun began to set, they reached the crest of a tall hill. Vesper reached the top first and pointed down the other side. Sarah was not used to this much hiking. The streets of New York had been much easier on her feet.

"There she is," Vesper called to Sarah. "It looks like the trolls haven't hurt her."

Even though her feet ached, Sarah sprinted up to join Vesper. She looked where he was pointing. There, she saw the statue. Sarah recognized the shape, the rays coming out of the statue's crown, and the uplifted hand with the torch. But this statue was only about fifty feet tall, much smaller than the one she knew, and all of it seemed to be carved from wood. It stood on the top of a broad, flat stone base that itself rose ten feet in the air.

She and Vesper found it much easier walking down the side of the hill, and soon were at the base of the statue. Sarah had been to her Statue of Liberty many times, and, clearly, so had whomever created this version. But Sarah noticed the face was different from the one she knew. Although parts of the sculpture seemed roughly carved, it seemed as if the artist had taken great care with the face.

"Isn't she beautiful?" said Vesper as he undid his pack.

"She sure is," said Sarah as she kept looking up. She seemed to recognize that face, but couldn't quite remember from where.

The sun started to set.

"We're here just in time," said Vesper.

Sarah looked around. There was no hut or house to be seen. "Where do we go?" she asked.

"Right here!" said Vesper, and he led Sarah to the back of the base of the statue. Vesper pushed in a section of the wall and a door swung open. "It's an old tracker spot," he said. "My father showed me once. If a tracker ever got stuck out here at night, he would know there was a safe, secret place to spend the night. The valley is filled with spots like this."

Vesper walked in first. Sarah peeked in, but it was very dark. Almost instantly, she saw something flutter out of the bushes. It glowed brightly against the night sky. "A sprite!" she said. The creature landed right on Sarah's open hand. Sarah looked closely. "It's Frieda!" she said. "She must have followed us!"

"I don't think so," said Vesper. "All sprites look alike."

Sarah didn't believe him. "Are you Frieda?" she said.

The sprite flew off her hand and did a somersault in the air.

"Aha!" said Sarah. "You should never doubt me," she told Vesper.

The gnome laughed as he took off his backpack.

With Frieda's light, they could see easily into the base of the statue. It seemed to have gone unharmed by passing trolls. There was a wood floor and three small beds in one corner, and a table and chairs in another. There was also a wooden ladder in the middle of the room that went up into the statue. Sarah saw that it was hollow. "You can peek out through the statue's crown," said Vesper. "It's a good lookout point."

After they entered, Vesper closed the secret panel tightly. There were no windows, so Sarah was glad to have Frieda, who sat herself on a rung of the ladder. Her light made a soft glow around the whole room.

"We can't make a fire for cooking," said Vesper while undoing his pack. "But I traded with Mazy for two loaves of Falala bread." Vesper dug into his pack and pulled out a package wrapped in a small cloth. It looked like the same material as Mazy's kerchief. He gave Sarah one loaf.

Vesper took a big bite. "Good," he said between mouthfuls, "but I would have added a bit more salt."

Sarah pulled off a little bit and tasted it. It was heavenly. It was soft on the inside, but the outside had a nice hard crunch. It reminded her of the bread she and her mother had bought every Sunday at Louie's Deli in the Bronx. She ate about half of the loaf and decided to save the rest for the morning. Before she did, she pulled off a bit and held it out to Frieda. Frieda zoomed down to see what Sarah had, but she just smiled and shook her head before she zoomed back to her post. Sarah wasn't sure what sprites ate, but it wasn't Falala bread.

Soon both Vesper and Sarah had bunked down for the night. Sarah had to scrunch up again to fit in the gnome-sized cot. In a short time, she heard the faint snores from her new friend who had quickly fallen asleep. Even Frieda's light had dimmed very low, and she seemed to have fallen asleep up on the ladder.

Sarah was having a hard time falling asleep. She thought about her parents and how worried they must be. She wondered if she and Vesper could do anything to help. Then Sarah thought she heard a noise outside, like a quiet moan. She looked at Vesper, but he just kept on snoring. Sarah tried to pretend she didn't hear it and scrunched down further under her blanket. She heard it again, louder this time—it sounded like someone or something was hurt.

Sarah got up and looked at the ladder, which rose up to the top of the statue. She looked at Vesper again, but he didn't move. She didn't want to wake Frieda, but the sprite jumped up the minute Sarah started climbing.

"Shhh," Sarah said. "Let's see if we can tell what it is."

Sarah slowly climbed the wooden ladder. She didn't like being in the statue. There was not a lot of room around her, which made her a bit claustrophobic, but Sarah climbed all the way to the top. It helped to have Frieda light the way. When Sarah reached the top, she could see there was a narrow slit that was cut all the way around the crown. She could see quite far along the surrounding hills.

Suddenly, near a bush, Sarah saw something lying on the ground about three hundred yards from the statue. She heard the moan again, and it seemed to be coming from the creature on the ground.

"Someone is hurt," Sarah told Frieda. She climbed down the ladder and went to Vesper. She nudged him in the shoulder.

"Vesper," she whispered, "some creature is hurt outside. I hear it moaning."

Vesper yawned and turned over. He rubbed his eyes. "It could be a troll," he said sleepily. "We are safe inside. Just go back to bed." And with that, the gnome rolled back over and quickly resumed his snoring.

Sarah laid in her cot. All was quiet for several minutes as she listened. Then she heard the moaning again. She thought of the troll trap she had seen.

She hopped up, grabbed her pack, and gently opened the secret panel. "Come on, Frieda," she said as the sprite flew down to her shoulder.

Sarah opened the door just enough for her and Frieda to get through. She closed it quietly as soon as they got outside. The night was a bit cold, but it was very clear. She saw the sky was filled with stars. Sarah and Frieda slowly made their way toward the sound. Sarah had grabbed the Dragon's Breath that Vesper had brought back from Mazy's. She held it out in front of her. Slowly, she inched closer to the groaning noise, which got louder as she approached. She could also smell a foul odor in the air. Finally, Sarah reached the bush she had seen from the crown. There, on the ground, lay a shadow. From its shape and smell, Sarah knew what it was. It was a troll, and it was hurt.

Sarah crept a bit closer, and the troll must have heard her, because he stopped moaning and tried to hide himself deeper under the bush.

Frieda flew into Sarah's face and shook her head. Sarah knew she was trying to tell her not to go on. But Sarah hated to see any creature hurt—even a loathsome creature like a troll.

When she bent down, the creature saw Sarah and bared its teeth. It growled and tried to lunge at her, but fell to the ground in pain. Sarah saw that the situation was just as she had guessed—the troll's foot was caught in a trap, and the chain on the trap was staked deeply into the ground.

Sarah stayed where she was. The smell was awful. She laid her pack down and sat on the ground herself.

"I won't hurt you," she said.

The troll was in too much pain to try to strike again. He just lay on the ground. Sarah could see the jaws of the trap clinging to his left foot, bits of blood running down and matting his thick fur.

Sarah inched a bit closer. Frieda flew into her face again, shook her head, and pointed back to the statue.

"You go, then," Sarah said. "I'm staying here."

Frieda did not fly away, but kept a worried look on her

face. Sarah was relieved that she did not leave—she felt braver with a friend nearby.

"I want to see if I can help you," said Sarah to the troll. "But you have to promise you won't hurt me."

The troll's glowing yellow eyes just stared at Sarah. She didn't know if she could trust him.

"I wonder if you really can talk," she said.

The creature looked at her. "Trolls talk," he groaned softly.

Sarah scampered back a little. Despite what Mazy had told her, she was surprised to hear the troll speak. He had a rough, gravelly voice.

"You can talk?" said Sarah. "I mean… I know you can talk. But you have to promise you won't hurt me."

The troll turned his head and sniffed. He wrinkled his nose and pointed at the Dragon's Breath.

"If you no hurt troll, why you have stink flower?" he said. Then he grabbed his foot and moaned again.

Sarah threw the flowers away behind her. "Better?" she said.

The troll sniffed again. He wriggled his nose. "You smell worse," he said.

Sarah stood up. "Well, you're no bed of roses," she snapped. She grabbed her pack and turned to leave.

"No go," groaned the troll. "Help troll. Help… *please.*"

Sarah turned back slowly.

"Promise you will not hurt me," she said.

The troll looked around. He seemed to be making sure there were no other trolls around.

"What is promise?" he asked.

Sarah thought for a minute. "A promise is when you say something and you mean it."

The troll seemed to understand. "Troll promise," he said "No hurt tall gnome."

Sarah laughed. "Gnomes think I'm a troll, and you think I'm a gnome. I can't win."

The troll sniffed. "What beast are you?"

"I'm the kind that can save you," she said. Sarah looked around and found a heavy branch. She edged closer to the troll. He pulled his leg away.

"How can I help unless you show me?" said Sarah. "You're as bad as a little kid."

The troll slowly slid his leg back near Sarah. She could see that the sharp jaws had dug deep into his foot.

"Not good," she said. "I think I can pry the trap open with the stick, but it will hurt a bit."

The troll pulled his leg back. "No hurt troll, no hurt troll," he whimpered.

"I'll try not to," said Sarah. "I promise."

The troll slid his leg back. Sarah pushed the stick between the jaws of the trap and pushed down. The troll moaned as the trap opened a little, but the stick broke in half.

"I need a bigger one," said Sarah.

Frieda flew off and zipped all around. She stopped and pointed to the ground near a tree. Sarah followed her and saw a bigger branch.

"Thanks, Frieda," she said. "I think that's just perfect."

She dragged the branch back and pried it between the jaws. Again, Sarah leaned on the stick, and the vise jaws of the trap opened—not by much, but enough this time for the troll to pull his foot out. Sarah stopped pressing and the trap instantly snapped shut.

The troll tried to stand, but moaned and fell to the ground.

"It will hurt for a while," said Sarah. She rummaged in her pack to see what she could find. Suddenly, Frieda zoomed away, and her light went with her.

"Frieda! Frieda!" said Sarah. "Come back!"

It was dark, but Sarah could still see well enough. She pulled out the rest of her loaf of bread and the kerchief it had been wrapped in.

"Here, eat this," she said as she handed the bread to the troll.

The troll greedily took it and stuffed it into his mouth.

Sarah took the kerchief and gently tied it around the wound on the troll's foot. "This will help stop the bleeding," she said. "All those years as a Girl Scout paid off."

The troll just looked at her.

Just then, Frieda zipped back and stopped by Sarah's face. In her tiny hands, she held five purple berries. Sarah recognized these as the ones Vesper had pointed out. He had said they helped aches and pains.

"Thanks, Frieda," said Sarah as she handed them to the troll. "These should help you, too."

The troll took the berries. He looked at Frieda and Sarah, put the berries in his mouth, and swallowed.

Sarah repacked her backpack. "What are you called?" she asked the troll.

The troll just looked at her.

"What is your name?" said Sarah. "What do the other trolls call you?"

"Trolls have no name," he said. "Just troll."

Sarah smiled. "Well, then, I think I'll give you one." She scratched her head. "You know, my mother always promised me a puppy," she mused. "But we lived in the city, and you can't really have dogs in the apartment building where I used to live…"

The troll looked at Sarah in confusion.

"But if I did get a dog," she continued, "I would have called him Ralph. So why don't I call you Ralph?"

The troll looked at her. "Ralph," he croaked.

Sarah wanted to ask the troll some tougher questions. She thought this was her best chance.

"Why do the trolls hate gnomes?" she asked.

The troll, now named Ralph, sneered. "Gnomes hate trolls!" he said. "They chase us with gnome blades. They set sharp traps for us. They hunt us in our woods. Trolls just want to live!"

Sarah had not thought of it that way before.

"But trolls have kidnapped all the gnomes!" she said. "Why?"

Ralph looked around. "Can't say," he said nervously. "Must leave!" The troll stood up and winced in pain, but he started to hobble away.

"Tell me!" said Sarah. "I helped you!"

Ralph stopped and turned to Sarah.

"Trolls not want to," he whispered. "Krickshap make trolls. Krickshap hurt trolls if we don't!"

"Who is Krickshap?" asked Sarah.

Ralph looked nervously around and started to hobble away. "Wait!" said Sarah, but Ralph did not stop. He only paused just before he got to the dense tree line.

"Trolls hate Krickshap!" he muttered before he disappeared into the forest.

CHAPTER 10

Mount Gnome

Sarah and Vesper had gotten up early and were already out on the road as the sun rose. Sarah had not told Vesper about the troll. She didn't want to upset him.

"We've made good time," said Vesper. "If we keep up this pace, we'll be at Mount Gnome by noon."

Sarah kept looking behind her. When they had woken up, she saw Frieda was gone. When she asked Vesper about it, he just shrugged. "Sprites come and go," he said. "I'm sure she'll be back."

Sarah liked her new friend. She hoped she would be back soon.

Throughout their hike, they passed many small villages and empty homes, and still they did not see any other gnomes. At one small stone house at the edge of a village, Vesper slowed. "This is my Uncle Rodzi's house," he said. He stopped to look inside. The furniture was all toppled, and items were thrown all around the floor.

"My uncle was very strong," said Vesper. "I bet he gave those trolls a fierce battle!"

Sarah thought of Ralph. "Vesper," she asked, "have you

ever heard the name Krickshap?"

Vesper thought a second. "No, never heard it before. Who or what is it?"

"I wish I knew," was all Sarah answered.

Just before noon, they came over the crest of a hill, and there it was—looming up on the horizon was a massive mountain unlike anything Sarah had ever seen. It was still some distance away, but Sarah could see the mountain was covered with many windows and doors. There were balconies carved into the side and terraces with gardens.

"It looks like a whole city inside a mountain," Sarah said.

Vesper looked proud. "It is!" he said. "And it's all done by gnomes—with the Ogg's guidance, of course."

Vesper pointed to a small window on one side. "That's where I live," he said. "It's a cozy place off the main kitchen."

They hurried now to get closer to the front entrance. It was a large arched entranceway carved of stone. It had the same carved work that Sarah had seen in the gnome-way door back at the potting shed. Just below it, she saw two carved statues of gnomes standing at attention. When they were sure no one was around, they ran to the entrance. Vesper stopped at the statues and looked sad as he rubbed his hand on one of the statues' shoulders. Sarah realized they were not carved statues, but real gnomes who had been turned to stone.

"Let's get inside before someone comes!" said Vesper.

But the air was already filled with an awful stench, and they knew it was too late.

Around the bend came a group of three trolls, all moaning because they were in the bright daylight. They were each using one hand to try to block their eyes from the bright sun. With their other hands, they dragged something behind them, bound in a net.

Vesper grabbed Sarah, and they ducked down behind a tree just in time. The trolls continued in through the archway and pushed open the main door. They were near enough now that Sarah could see what they were dragging. It was a gnome, and it was putting up a terrible fight. It kept kicking and screaming at the trolls.

"Let me go, you furry hairballs!"

It was Mazy.

The trolls dragged in their captive, then slammed the door shut. Sarah and Vesper heard locks being turned.

"I can't believe they got Mazy," said Sarah.

"That's strange," said Vesper. "I have *never* seen trolls out in the daylight. Something or someone must be behind this."

Sarah looked at Vesper. "Krickshap," she said. Then Sarah told him about what she had done last night and what she had learned.

"You did what?" Vesper yelled.

"I think the trolls are being forced to kidnap gnomes," she said.

"You could have been killed!" Vesper said. "And no troll needs to be told to act badly," he added. "It's the way they are."

Sarah wasn't sure, but didn't want to argue. She walked up to the front door and pulled the large wooden handle. It was shut tight.

"I guess we don't get in," she said.

Vesper laughed. "This is just the front entrance," he said. "There are many other ways to get in."

"But won't all the other entrances be locked or guarded?" asked Sarah.

"Not if the trolls don't know about them," said Vesper, as he started on a small path that led around the mountain.

CHAPTER 11

A Way In

Sarah followed Vesper through the underbrush that encircled the whole base of the mountain. She had a hard time keeping up with him. He seemed to know the way very well. At last, they stopped by a boulder that was tucked into the side of the mountain.

"Here's where we get in," said Vesper.

Sarah looked at the boulder, then all around her. She didn't see any way inside.

"Okay, I give up," she said. "How do we get in?"

Vesper laughed. "Grab one side of the boulder and help me push it."

He and Sarah pushed, and the boulder rolled gently aside—there, Sarah saw a round hole leading up into the mountain.

"A tunnel," said Sarah.

"Even better," said Vesper. "It's a gnome-way, and it leads right to the main kitchen."

"I thought all gnome-ways had carved wooden doors covering them," Sarah said.

"Some do, some don't," the gnome answered. "There are

hundreds carved into stone walls, trees, and even mountains like this one."

"Who built them all?" Sarah asked.

Vesper rested by the tunnel entrance. "No one knows," he said. "They have always been here, even before the Ogg. We call them gnome-ways because we use them all the time."

Sarah looked in the tunnel. It was as black and dark as the one in the potting shed. "How do you know where they all go?"

"Ah," said Vesper. "Trial and error, mostly. Many of the gnome-ways just lead you to other places in Oglinoth or the surrounding towns. But some lead to faraway places."

"Like to my world," said Sarah.

"Yes," said Vesper. "All the ones that lead to the upper world—I mean, your world—can only be opened with keys."

"Why is that?" asked Sarah.

"Because not all of the gnome-ways to your world open up in such a friendly place," Vesper said. "Some open up at the tops of frozen mountains, or in the middle of steaming hot deserts. I even heard that one opens up at a cliff, and if you were to pop through that doorway, you'd fall down a thousand-foot drop. We were losing a lot of over-curious gnomes."

"I think keeping them locked sounds like a good idea," said Sarah.

Just then, two trolls came around from the side of the hill, each carrying a squirming sack.

"Stay down," said Vesper as he and Sarah ducked down under the bushes.

Sarah heard clucking and could tell that the bags were filled with chickens that the trolls must have found in the countryside. Even if the trolls could see Sarah and Vesper, they paid no attention. They each held a sack with one hand while they shielded their eyes with the other. They moaned as they walked quickly. Sarah could tell they did not like being out in the sun. Soon the trolls passed out of sight.

"We'd better get inside," said Vesper. "Just follow me."

Vesper climbed into the tunnel. As soon as he entered Sarah heard a loud WHOOSH and saw Vesper get sucked up and away.

"Hey, wait for me!" she called as she also crawled inside. Immediately, her whole body was pulled up into the mountain. It felt funny to Sarah to be falling up instead of down.

In less than a minute, she came gently tumbling out the other end. She looked around; she was in a great-sized room. There were no lights on, but Sarah could see around her. She stood up. The ceilings were very high—almost fifteen feet tall, she thought. Around her were a half-dozen long wooden tables, with broken bowls and utensils all scattered about. She also saw what looked like cooking stoves—maybe five or six altogether. They were littered with dirty cooking pots and stale bread. Sarah sniffed. She smelled the recognizable odor of troll, but also the smells of rotten vegetables and moldy cheese. There, in the center of the room, was Vesper. His eyes were filled with tears.

"Will you look what they did to my kitchen!" he muttered to Sarah, once she came over. He went over to the stove and looked at one of the pots. It was filled with rotten food. "How can anyone treat a kitchen like this?" he said.

They heard a growl and quickly hid behind one of the massive, cold stoves. They had just gotten themselves hidden when in strode a plump troll, carrying a large pan in his hand.

"Treat troll badly," he muttered to himself. "Krickshap mean to troll. Krickshap try cooking own food!" The troll dumped the pan on one of the tables, turned, and left.

Vesper and Sarah watched the troll leave before they came out of their hiding spot.

"Trolls cooking in *my* kitchen!" he said. "Don't they have any respect?"

"Yes, yes," said Sarah. "But we're not here to save your pots and pans, are we?"

That seemed to snap Vesper back into action. "Right. Of course not!" he said. "Let's see if we can find where they are keeping all the others!"

But as they snuck out of the kitchen, Sarah couldn't help but notice Vesper as he looked at an overturned pot on the floor and grimaced.

CHAPTER 12

An Army of Stone

Because he had lived in Mount Gnome, Vesper knew all the safest ways to traverse the mountain. They heard many trolls walking about, and on several occasions, they had to duck into a hallway or jump behind a door before they were seen. It was a good thing they could smell the trolls long before they could see them. Sarah saw rooms that looked like art galleries, with gnome paintings still on some of the walls. They looked into bedrooms and saw that the small beds and desks were all overturned. Nowhere did they find a single gnome.

"There must be a lot of gnomes being held prisoner," said Sarah. "And they are probably keeping them all together."

Vesper rubbed his long beard as he thought. "The only place big enough to keep everyone would be the great concert hall," said Vesper. "Come on!"

He led Sarah down a long, winding stone staircase to a floor below. They entered a wide hallway and Vesper pointed at the wooden double doors at the end. The hallway was empty. They sniffed. No trolls anywhere nearby. They ran up to the doors and listened. All was quiet. Sarah looked at the doors and noticed they were elaborately carved; they had the same leaf borders she had seen before, but the rest of the door was carved with instruments and musical notes. There was even the face of a gnome carved in the center of one panel.

"That's the Ogg," said Vesper, when he noticed what Sarah was looking at.

Sarah looked at the face again. Even though it was carved out of wood, Sarah could tell that it was a kind face with a big smile.

"I don't think they're inside," said Vesper. "There's no noise. And no guards."

Sarah and Vesper each grabbed one of the large handles and pulled the great doors open.

"NO!" said Vesper, once he saw what was inside. He fell to his knees and pounded the wooden floor.

Sarah looked around. What she saw shocked her. The room was filled with hundreds of gnomes, and all of them had been turned to stone. No wonder there weren't any guards—they knew none of their prisoners could run away.

Vesper got up and ran in. He searched through the statues. He seemed to know them all.

"Pichard… Grindall… Hobart," he said as he touched each of his friends. "Here's Moontooth… Heelis… and old man McKee." Then Vesper stopped when he got to two statues that stood off to the side. Even though they had been turned to stone, Sarah could tell that they looked like Vesper. Vesper put his arms around them both and hugged them.

"Mom... Dad..." he said. "I've missed you so much."

Sarah came over and hugged Vesper. "I knew you would find them."

"When I was stone, I could still sense what was around me," Vesper said. He looked at their faces again and leaned in close. "Know this," he said. "I will save you both."

Sarah looked around the room. It was filled with statues in every corner, except for an open space against the far back wall. Sarah made her way there.

"Vesper," she called. "Come here!"

He ran to the back of the room to join his friend. When Vesper got there, Sarah pointed at the open space on the floor.

There, in a huge pile, lay hundreds of swords. All were individually made and were different shapes and sizes, but Sarah knew what they were.

"The swords of the gnomes," she said.

"They just left them here?" said Vesper.

"I guess they knew the gnomes couldn't get to them," said Sarah. She suddenly was reminded of the troll she had named Ralph. "Besides, trolls hate gnome blades. I don't think they wanted to touch them any more than they had to."

"Well, that's good luck for us!" said Vesper, as he picked up several swords and started examining each one.

Sarah picked one up and looked it over. It looked a lot like Vesper's, but it had more of a curved handle, and small triangular marks were cut into the side of the blade. Sarah went over to the nearest statue and slipped it into the stone sheath on the gnome's side. She waited. Nothing happened.

"What's wrong?" she asked Vesper.

Vesper came over, pulled the sword back out, and looked at it.

"Each sword is made for only one gnome," he said, as he looked at the face of the statue next to him. "This is Oslo of Oglinoth. He's a musician. He would never own a blade like this." Vesper held the sword up so Sarah could see it. "The curved blade is used by farmers when they cut wheat," he said. "And look at these three marks on the blade. That's the symbol of the Gringus clan. So this sword is from someone in that family. And judging by the weight, I would guess it's probably the sword of Pa Gringus."

Sarah was impressed. "Well, let's start getting these back to their rightful owners!"

"I think not!" commanded a menacing voice from the front entrance of the room.

Sarah and Vesper dropped the swords in surprise and looked up. There, in the doorway, stood a half-dozen angry-looking trolls. In the center, towering above them, stood a creature Sarah had never seen before. He was hunched over, but if he stood up straight, Sarah guessed he would be over eight feet tall. He was extremely thin and bony. He smiled meanly at Sarah, and she could see that his ears were pointy and had tufts of hair growing out from each. He wore a long, black, flowing robe, with a cape draped over one shoulder. On his head was a metal crown, and in his bony hand, he held a scepter with a golden orb on the top.

"I see we have company," he said in a high-pitched voice.

Vesper whispered, "It's an elf."

Sarah stared at the creature. "Krickshap!" she said.

CHAPTER 13

Krickshap

Krickshap pushed the trolls aside and strode into the room.

"I usually have to send my lazy trolls outside to capture gnomes," he said. "But it was nice of you both to save me the trouble."

The elf poked his scepter into the back of the nearest troll. It shocked the creature with a surge of electricity. The troll moaned in pain.

"Take their swords and let them turn to stone like the others!" Krickshap yelled.

All the trolls started advancing on Sarah and Vesper. The elf turned to leave.

Sarah tried to think of something to do. Vesper was slowly reaching for his sword. Sarah had an idea.

"Wait," she yelled. "We can help you!"

Vesper looked at Sarah. "I would rather fight!" he whispered.

"There are too many of them," Sarah whispered back. "How can you help your family if you are turned back to stone?"

Vesper eased his hand back off his sword.

Krickshap turned and walked back into the room. "How can two gnomes be of help to me?"

Sarah moved forward. "My friend here is a great chef," she said. "I am sure he can make you better meals than you're used to!"

Krickshap rubbed his chin with his bony hand. "Trolls are not good for much," he groaned. "Especially not for cooking."

Krickshap moved forward and looked Sarah over. "You look too tall for a gnome," he said as he pointed at her. "And you carry no sword. What kind of creature are you?"

"I am a human," said Sarah.

"Human!" said the elf. "I have heard that humans are good storytellers. Is this true?"

Vesper spoke up. "Yes— Sarah is a great storyteller," he said. "She knows all the best human stories!"

Sarah looked at Vesper. She did love to read, and she wanted to be a writer when she grew up.

Krickshap smiled. "Very well," he snapped. "Take the gnome to the kitchen. Let's see what he

can do." He poked Vesper in the chest. "But if your meals are no better than the trolls', I'll turn you to stone *and* break you into a million pieces." He turned to Sarah. "Take this one to the cell with the other prisoner," he snapped at the trolls surrounding her. "I will listen to a story with my lunch."

Three trolls grabbed Vesper and hustled him away toward the kitchens. The others grabbed Sarah, moved her down the hall, and stopped by a doorway that had a gate latched across it. One troll took a key from the outside wall and opened the lock. The gate screeched as it slowly slid open, and the trolls pushed Sarah inside. The gate clanged as it was shut and locked again.

The trolls left, and Sarah looked around. It was very dark in the room. She remembered what Krickshap had said. *Take this one to the cell with the other prisoner.* Sarah moved slowly into the room as her eyes got used to the dark. It was then that she realized that there really was someone else there—in the back on a cot lay a figure.

Sarah moved closer. The figure's eyes opened and looked at Sarah. It slowly sat up in the cot. Sarah could see a face etched with wrinkles and a big, bushy, white beard. He smiled as he looked at Sarah, and she recognized his face as the one she'd seen carved into the concert hall doors.

"Are you the Ogg?" she asked.

CHAPTER 14

The Ogg

"I am," the figure said. The Ogg stood up slowly and bowed to Sarah. "I have not met a human for a very long time," he said. He gestured for Sarah to come closer. Sarah could see that the Ogg was indeed much taller than the other gnomes; he seemed as tall as Sarah's father, but much rounder. Although his clothes seemed ripped and patched in places, he wore the same style of clothing as Vesper. Sarah noticed that he also wore a black belt with a brass buckle. The letters O.G.G. were etched in its center.

"Please, have a seat," the Ogg said. "I wish I could offer you some lemonade, but I'm afraid I don't have much here."

Sarah sat down on a small wooden stool.

"My name's Sarah," she said. A million questions ran through her head. "What happened down here?" she blurted. "When did Krickshap come? How come he didn't turn you to stone? Vesper and I were worried…"

"Vesper!" interrupted the Ogg as he clapped his hands together. "You came with Vesper? That means he is okay!"

Sarah stood up. "Yes," she said. "Vesper is fine. He was sent to cook for Krickshap. We just came through the gnome-way to try and help."

The Ogg sat down. "It was a mistake to send Vesper away," he said, "but he was our last hope."

"What happened?" asked Sarah.

The Ogg rubbed his bushy white beard. "We had lived in peace for many years. We had always had trouble with the trolls, but nothing too bad. Suddenly, the trolls started banding together and raiding our homes. They didn't just steal food, but started capturing gnomes. I sent our trackers to see what they could find, but they never returned. Then we learned about Krickshap!"

"What does he want?" asked Sarah.

"Who knows?" said the Ogg. "But whatever it is, it's no good."

"Are all elves bad?" Sarah asked.

"No, not at all," said the Ogg. "But elves tend to live quite far away, in distant forests. We usually don't run into many of them. I think Krickshap is what we call a bad seed. He was probably thrown out from the elf world, and is now trying to take over ours."

"With the help of the trolls," said Sarah.

The Ogg thought for a minute.

"We were never kind to the trolls," he said sadly. "Maybe Krickshap was good to them at first, to gain their confidence. But you've probably seen how mean he is to them now. I think they do what he says out of fear."

Sarah thought of Ralph. "I know they do," she said.

"Almost all the gnomes had been captured," continued

the Ogg. "There were a small handful of us left, and Vesper volunteered to go through a gnome-way to try and find help."

Sarah felt embarrassed. "I guess that 'help' would be me," she said. "But a lot of good I've been."

The Ogg put his arm around Sarah. "Nonsense," he said. "If Vesper believes in you, then so do I."

Sarah blushed.

"I sent Vesper through a very special gnome-way," the Ogg said. "Do you live near the house at the entrance?"

"More than near," said Sarah. "I live *in* the house, with my parents."

"You do!" the Ogg said. "Good for you!" He smiled widely. It was now he who had many questions. "Do the gardens still look good? How is the house? Does the dining-room ceiling still have a leak in it?"

Sarah stared at the Ogg. "Well… I don't really know," she said. "I just moved in the day before yesterday with my parents. I think it's been sitting empty for a long time."

The Ogg frowned. "Too bad, too bad," he said. "That house is a great house. It has good bones to it. Maybe your parents will fix it up!"

Sarah thought of her father and his bandaged thumb. "Maybe," said Sarah, wondering why the Ogg would care so much about a house in her world. Just then, Sarah noticed the scabbard on the Ogg's side. There was no sword in it.

"They took your sword?" said Sarah.

The Ogg smiled at her with a twinkle in his eye—the kind of smile that shows someone understands a secret. "Yes," he said. "They took it from me a long time ago."

Sarah gently poked the Ogg in his big round belly. "Pretty soft for stone," she said.

The Ogg laughed. "Only true gnomes turn to stone when they lose their swords," he said.

"And you are not a gnome," guessed Sarah. "You are human, just like me!"

CHAPTER 15

Many Answers

Sarah thought of something she had done days before. She felt inside her sweatshirt pocket. She was surprised that after everything she had been through, it was still there—a small oval picture in a frame, the one she found in the potting shed. She pulled it out and looked at the picture of the farmer and his wife. Then she looked up at the Ogg. The farmer's face may have looked younger, and his beard had been black then, but Sarah could tell it was the same person. She turned the frame over and saw the two names written in the cursive handwriting: Otis Gregory Grimwald and Lavenia Sally Grimwald. She handed the frame to the Ogg.

"Otis Gregory Grimwald," she said, "That's your name. And your initials are O.G.G.!"

The Ogg took the picture from Sarah and looked at it lovingly.

"This was taken on our wedding day," he said as he rubbed his finger over the frame. "I had just spent a year building the house before we moved into it."

Sarah was confused. "But if you are a human," she said, "why did you end up here? Where is your wife?"

The Ogg stopped looking at the picture and turned to Sarah. "Lavenia is dead," he said.

"I'm sorry," said Sarah.

The Ogg smiled. "It was a long time ago, Sarah," he added. "We lived many years in that house. I worked the farm, and Lavenia grew the vegetables. We were very happy."

"What happened?" asked Sarah.

"Smallpox," said the Ogg. "Took half the town with it. Lavenia came down with it in June. By September, she was gone."

"That must have been very hard on you," said Sarah.

"It was," he said. "I barely went out of the house all winter. But when spring came, the birds returned, the flowers bloomed, and I knew I had to get back to work on the farm. Lavenia would have wanted that."

"How did you end up here?" asked Sarah.

"Ah, yes," said the Ogg. "I had been digging a new garden in the yard, when I discovered a deep hole in the ground."

"A gnome-way?" asked Sarah.

"The same one you came through," said the Ogg. "I discovered this wonderful world down here. The gnomes were very friendly to me," he added, "but they were barely surviving. They didn't know how to grow their own food or how to build a home. I would go back home again and return with tools, books, food—anything that would help them. Soon I was spending so much time down here, it just made sense for me to stay." The Ogg rubbed his belt buckle. "Lavenia gave me this when we got married," he said.

"The gnomes would always see me wearing it and started calling me the Ogg, or the One Great Gnome. They made me one of them, and I was deeply moved."

"Vesper said you carved the Statue of Liberty," said Sarah. "Is that Lavenia's face?"

The Ogg laughed. "I did that for my own enjoyment," he said. "The gnomes saw how much it meant to me, and they have always treated it as a honored place."

"Why did you build the potting shed over the gnome-way?" Sarah asked.

"To keep it hidden!" said the Ogg. "We know what humans are like! They would have ruined this world."

Sarah knew the Ogg was right. How long until humans tried to put up fast-food restaurants in every town?

"Vesper said there are gnome-ways all over the place," said Sarah.

"There are, there are," said the Ogg. "They've been here long before the gnomes. Don't know who built them. Many lead to the upper world, but some go to dangerous places. You can't get rid of a gnome-way, but I've had the bad ones boarded up."

Sarah was glad to be getting all these answers. "Did the gnomes use the gnome-ways regularly to come to my world—I mean, our world?"

"Not very often," said the Ogg. "The gnomes were always afraid of humans—too tall, too busy all the time. But we did have that one large clan who moved to your world."

"Moved!" said Sarah. "Permanently?"

The Ogg laughed. "Oh, and I bet you've heard about them, too!"

Sarah seemed confused.

"They all took the gnome-way that led to Ireland," said the Ogg. "They loved the place, and decided to stay. The men even shaved their white beards to try and blend into the woods more. They still stay out of the way of humans, but some have been seen. Humans have even made up stories about them."

Sarah thought she understood, and smiled. "Leprechauns are really gnomes?" she said.

"Absolutely!" the Ogg said with a wink.

Just then, two trolls came up to the iron gate in front of their cell. One of them grabbed the key and opened the lock. He beckoned for Sarah to follow him. Sarah looked at the Ogg.

"Better go," said the Ogg. "You never want to keep an angry elf waiting."

CHAPTER 16

The Story

Sarah was brought to a great hall. The walls were lined with beautiful tapestries. Sarah could see the ornate scenes that were sewn into them. They seemed to tell the history of the gnomes. She saw tapestries of gnomes living in caves, of the Ogg arriving, and many more with scenes of everyday life. The trolls walked her to the very front of the hall. Sarah could see a tall chair with a figure in it. The chair looked just like the one Vesper's father had carved for the Ogg. Krickshap was sitting in it, his shoulders and head hunched over. He held his scepter in one bony hand. Behind him hung the largest, most beautiful tapestry. It showed a scene of the Ogg and Lavenia standing next to their house. Sarah remembered that scene from the photo she had found.

"Ah, I see my entertainment has arrived," Krickshap said. He turned to one of the trolls that brought Sarah in. "Where is my lunch?" he demanded. "Go get it before I give you some of this!" He waved his scepter with the golden orb at the trembling troll, who turned and ran from the room.

Krickshap eyed Sarah up and down. "So you're a human girl," he said. "Nothing very special."

Sarah bit her lip. She wanted to give him an earful, but decided to be quiet and see what would happen.

The first troll hurried back in, with Vesper alongside him. Vesper carried a tray with a large soup bowl on top.

The elf gestured for Vesper to come closer. Vesper looked at Sarah standing there and brought the tray up to Krickshap.

"What is this?" Krickshap said with a scowl. He leaned his long head over and grabbed the tray and sniffed the steam that was rising from the bowl.

"It's cream-of-beetroot soup," said Vesper. "That kitchen was a mess. It's not like I had a lot to work with… "

"Quiet!" snapped Krickshap. "Hmmmm… it smells good." He took the spoon off the tray and scooped up a tiny bit of soup. He stopped just as it reached his mouth and pushed the spoon toward Sarah.

"Taste this," he said. "I want to be sure he's not trying to poison me."

"Poison?" Vesper interrupted. "I am a chef! I would never put poison in one of my meals!"

Krickshap grabbed his scepter with his free hand and poked Vesper with its golden orb. The shock knocked Vesper to the ground.

"No!" yelled Sarah as she ran to Vesper's side.

Krickshap just laughed, slowly scooped a spoonful of soup, and held it out to Sarah. "Taste this, or I'll give him another jolt!"

Sarah helped Vesper up and walked over to Krickshap. She took the spoon and smelled the soup. It did smell good. She opened her mouth and swallowed it all in one gulp.

Sarah smiled at Vesper. "That's really good," she said.

"Of course," said Vesper, who seemed a bit dizzy but otherwise okay. "Just think what I could do with the right ingredients."

"Enough!" said the elf. "Take the gnome to the cell," he said to his trolls. "I want to hear my story in peace."

The trolls escorted Vesper out of the room. He was a bit wobbly on his feet, but still smiled at Sarah before he left. Krickshap threw the spoon down and brought the bowl to his mouth. Sarah was disgusted as he poured all the soup down his throat in big gulps. Some of it splattered out and ran down his robe. He dropped the empty bowl to the ground and wiped his mouth on his sleeve, then let out a loud belch.

"So gnomes *are* good for something," he said. "Now tell me a story!"

Sarah felt nervous. She loved reading and knew tons of stories, but she didn't know what kind of story an elf would like. "Well," she said, stalling, "what kind of story would you like to hear?"

"GOLD!" snapped Krickshap. "Tell me a story about the gnomes' gold, and where they have hidden it!"

Sarah was surprised. "Gold?" she said. "I haven't heard anything about gnomes having gold."

"Of course they have gold!" said Krickshap. "They just have it hidden. But I'll find it."

Sarah noticed that the elf had begun to seem a bit dizzy. She wasn't sure if the talk of gold had upset him, but he didn't look well.

"Now begin!" said Krickshap as he eased himself back into his chair.

Sarah cleared her throat. "Once upon a time," she began, thinking quickly, "there was a gnome who had a giant mountain of gold!"

Sarah didn't get any further. She stopped when she heard the sound of loud snoring. They were coming from Krickshap. He had fallen asleep.

CHAPTER 17

Friends

Sarah didn't understand what had happened, but she wasn't going to take any chances. She ran out of the room and found her way back to the cell. Luckily, there were no trolls around. She saw Vesper and the Ogg behind the gate. They were both smiling.

"He fell asleep fast!" Vesper said.

"How did you know?" asked Sarah.

The Ogg smiled. "Cream-of-beetroot soup!" he laughed. "Puts anyone right to sleep."

Sarah was mad at herself for not figuring that out. "But you said you would never put anything bad in your meals," she said.

"And I meant it," said Vesper. "We use cream-of-beetroot soup when we can't sleep at night. I was lucky to find all the ingredients."

Sarah realized something. "But I had a sip," she said. "And I don't feel sleepy."

"That's because you just had one spoonful," said Vesper. "It takes at least a cupful to really knock you out."

The Ogg rattled the cell door. "Beetroot soup would

knock a gnome out for the whole night, but I don't know how long it works on an elf. We better get out of here before he wakes up."

Sarah looked on the wall where the key was kept. It was not there.

"The troll guard must have taken it with him," said Sarah.

Vesper pulled his sword from his side and tried to pick the lock with it.

Sarah looked at Vesper's sword, then at the empty scabbard on the side of the Ogg. She looked worried.

The Ogg sensed what was concerning her. "It's okay, Sarah," he said. "All the gnomes know that I am really human."

"Born human, yes," Vesper answered, still trying to pry open the lock, "but you will never find a better gnome."

"I know why Krickshap is here," said Sarah. "He's looking for all your gold!"

The Ogg and Vesper both looked at each other and groaned.

"We have no gold," said the Ogg. "I never understand why people think that."

"What about the leprechauns?" asked Sarah. "Don't they collect gold?"

"Hogwash," said Vesper. "Just old tales. We have better things to do around here than run about looking for gold."

"You're correct," said the Ogg as he rubbed his beard. "But if Krickshap is looking for gold, maybe we can use that to our advantage."

"How?" asked Sarah.

The Ogg smiled. "I have no idea… yet."

While the friends had been talking, they had not noticed a shadowy figure slowly creeping down the hall towards them. Vesper saw him first from the corner of his eye.

"Watch out, Sarah," he said as he took his sword from the lock and waved it at the approaching figure. "It's a troll!"

Sarah had no place to run, so she stood her ground. The troll did not run. He slowly walked toward Sarah. She noticed he had a slight limp, as if one of his feet had been hurt. Sarah looked closely at the stranger's furry face. She thought he looked familiar.

"Ralph?" she said. "Is that you?" Sarah started to walk toward the troll.

"No, Sarah," said Vesper. "He'll kill you!"

As Sarah got closer, the troll stopped. It was hard to see his face through all that fur, but Sarah thought she saw him smile. He still smelled pretty bad.

"Ralph! It *is* you!" she said as she ran the rest of the way up to him. "How is your leg?"

"Better," he grunted. He looked past Sarah at the two gnomes in the cell. Vesper still had his sword pointing at him.

"Vesper, put that away," she said. "You are scaring Ralph."

Even though Vesper had heard the story of Sarah's meeting with the troll, he was still astounded. He kept his sword out.

"He's a troll!" Vesper said. "You can't trust him!"

The Ogg gently put his arm on Vesper. "I think Sarah knows what she is saying," he said. "We are not in danger from this troll."

Vesper felt unsure, but lowered his sword.

"Come on," said Sarah as she put her arm around Ralph. "Come meet my friends."

Ralph still stared at the sword and did not move. "Hate gnome blades," he said. "Gnomes try to kill trolls with gnome blades."

Vesper slowly put his sword into its scabbard. Ralph let Sarah lead him over to the bearded gnomes in the cage, but he stayed behind her.

"Ralph," she said, "these are my friends. This is the Ogg and Vesper."

Ralph just stared at them.

Sarah moved closer to Vesper. "It's polite to shake hands when you are introduced," she whispered.

"Shake hands with a troll!" said Vesper. "I'd rather kiss Krickshap!"

Ralph bared his yellow teeth and growled at Vesper.

It was the Ogg who eased the tension. He extended his arm through the cage. "It's nice to meet you, Ralph," he said.

Ralph looked at his outstretched hand and sniffed it. He looked at Sarah.

"Go on," she said.

Ralph reached out a furry paw, and he and the Ogg shook.

Just then, they heard a door open and slam shut, then heard the sound of footsteps headed their way.

Quickly, Ralph let go of the Ogg and stood behind Sarah, grabbing her roughly.

"It's a trap," said Vesper. "I knew it!"

Two trolls came down the hall and stopped when they saw Ralph holding Sarah. They ran toward him and growled in a language Sarah had never heard. Ralph answered them back in the same rough speech. One of the trolls was carrying the key, and he went to open the cage. Vesper reached for his sword, but the Ogg gently held him back. Vesper didn't know what was going on, but he stayed still.

The troll opened the gate, and Ralph pushed Sarah in. The guard locked the door again and, this time, hung the keys on the wall. Ralph and the two guards talked to each other in their language for a bit, then Ralph said something that made the two guards laugh. They were still laughing as they walked out of the room, leaving Ralph alone to guard the prisoners.

When everything was quiet again, Ralph reached up and grabbed the keys and unlocked the gate. "Sorry for pushing," he said, "but had to tell them Krickshap sent me to put you here."

Sarah, Vesper, and the Ogg walked out of the cell.

"Smart thinking, Ralph," said Sarah. "You saved us."

Vesper starred at Ralph, then looked at the Ogg and at Sarah. He slowly extended his hand to Ralph.

"Thank you," said Vesper.

Ralph sniffed his hand, then shook it, as he had done with the Ogg.

"We better get out of here before they come back," said the Ogg. They started making their way down a back hall.

"Tell me, Ralph," said Sarah. "What did you say to them to make them laugh?"

"I say they better let me guard you alone," Ralph said.

"Why?" asked Vesper.

"I said I had cold," said Ralph. "So I couldn't smell your awful stench."

"What?!" said Vesper, a bit too loudly. "We don't smell!"

"Quiet!" said Sarah. "Let's just get going."

This time, when Sarah looked at Ralph, she definitely saw him smiling.

CHAPTER 18

Escape

The four friends quietly ran down a back staircase. The Ogg took the lead, with Vesper right behind him. Sarah was easily able to keep up, but she kept stopping to help Ralph. The stairs were not easy on his hurt foot. At the end of the staircase, they came to a landing with no doors or windows.

"No exit," said Sarah. "We better go back."

The Ogg and Vesper looked at each other. Then Vesper went up to a crevice in the stone wall and gently pushed on it with both hands. A secret doorway in the stone creaked and swung open.

"Good going, Vesper," said the Ogg. "I think you know this place better than I do."

Vesper and the Ogg climbed in through the doorway and gestured for Sarah and Ralph to follow.

"Is it way outside?" asked Ralph as he tried to see past them.

"No," said the Ogg, smiling. "We can't fight Krickshap alone. We need an army."

Sarah climbed in and instantly knew where she was. It was the great concert hall, and she was looking at the army of stone gnomes.

Ralph peeked in and growled. "No go in there," he said. "Two gnomes enough."

Sarah held his paw. "It's okay, Ralph," she said. "We won't let anyone hurt you."

"Of course not," added the Ogg.

Ralph still looked uneasy and just stood by the doorway.

Vesper was already gathering up as many swords as he could off the floor. He set them with a clatter on a large oak table, then handed one to the Ogg.

"Once we return each sword to its proper owner," Vesper said, "we'll have an army of gnomes to help stop Krickshap."

Sarah looked at the mass of swords on the table and the even bigger pile still littering the floor. "Won't that take a long time?" she said.

"Not for a gnome," said the Ogg. He looked at the first sword. It was a thick, broad sword with a crescent moon carved into the handle. "Shaped for a woodcutter," said the Ogg. "And the moon shape says it belongs to the Moontooth family!"

Vesper hurried through the rows of statues.

"Here is Mayfield Moontooth," said Vesper, stopping at a small, broad sized gnome in the center of the room.

Sarah and the Ogg ran over. The Ogg took the sword and slid it into the sheath at the side of the statue. Instantly, the statue started bouncing, just as Vesper had done when Sarah had given him back his sword. The stone seemed to melt away, and in a few seconds Mayfield Moontooth stood groggily, alive again. He blinked and stared at the people in front of him.

"Welcome back, Mayfield," said the Ogg, patting him on the back.

Mayfield looked around as if he was trying to remember what had happened to him. Suddenly it all came back to him. "It's the trolls," he said in a gruff, low voice. "They grabbed me in the woods and took my sword!" Mayfield stopped when he noticed Sarah. "A beastie!" he said as he reached for his sword.

Vesper grabbed his hand. "Easy, Moontooth," he said, smiling. "She's no beastie. She's one of us."

"We can explain it all," said the Ogg, "but first we need to help the others."

Vesper grabbed the next sword. "Narrow blade, leather handle. I think that's a Borgalum sword."

"Right here," called the Ogg. "Rumphus Borgalum, I believe."

The same thing happened to Rumphus as had happened to Moontooth; after a second or two, he recovered, and after a dizzy moment or two, he was ready to help. Each newly-freed gnome quickly grabbed other swords to help their friends. Soon dozens of gnomes were freed, with dozens more coming around every few seconds. Sarah quickly explained to them what had happened and told them about Krickshap. In turn, the gnomes told each of their newly freed friends.

Then Sarah noticed a familiar face that was just coming back to life. She put her arm around the groggy gnome.

"Hello, Mazy," she said. "Nice to see you again."

Mazy smiled at her. "Nice to see a friendly face."

"How did they capture you?" asked Sarah. "You were always so careful."

Mazy blushed and looked a bit embarrassed. "Had me a little picnic by the lake," she said. "Ate too much and fell asleep. Next thing I knew, I had a net over me and was being dragged along the ground."

"Well, you're with friends again," said Sarah.

Vesper had finished up with all the swords he had grabbed. The Ogg met him and handed him two more. "I thought you would like to do these," he said.

Vesper looked at the blades. They were quite large and shaped like axes.

"Tracker swords, I think," said the Ogg, grinning.

Vesper looked at the handles. They both had two stars and a moon carved into the side, just like his.

"Thanks," said Vesper as he carried the swords to the two statues he had seen before. He slid the first into its sheath, then quickly slid in the other.

Just as the others had, the two statues shook and jumped, and the stone seemed to melt away. In a few seconds, the freed gnomes drowsily looked at their rescuer.

"Mom! Dad!" said Vesper as he hugged them both.

After a few minutes of catching up, crying, and hugging, the Ogg came over.

"Well, that's everyone," he said, smiling, as he slid his own sword into its scabbard. He turned and looked over the heads of almost five hundred gnomes. "It's time to take back our mountain."

Just then, Vesper's father noticed something moving by the back doorway.

"It's a troll!" he yelled as he started running toward him. "I'll enjoy running him through myself!"

Several gnomes shouted their agreement and followed him, all with their swords in the air. Ralph, who had been standing by the doorway the whole time, saw the angry crowd advancing toward him and ran away.

Vesper caught up with his father and held him back. "No, Dad!" said Vesper. "I know it's hard to believe, but he's our friend."

Sarah ran out the doorway and looked up the staircase. Ralph was gone.

CHAPTER 19

Two Armies

Sarah told the gnomes about Ralph and how he had helped them escape. There was a lot of grumbling in the crowd.

"Never heard of a troll who would help a gnome," said one.

"Only good troll is a dead one," someone laughed.

"Enough!" yelled Sarah. "Krickshap is the enemy."

The Ogg moved to the front of the crowd and opened the large carved doors. "Sarah is right," he said. "Our job is to get rid of one troublesome elf. Let's go!"

And with that, five hundred gnomes and one girl charged out into the hallway and up the stairs.

As they entered the great hall, they were met by another army. The hall was filled with hundreds of trolls, who growled and bared their crooked yellow teeth at the oncoming gnomes. Behind the trolls stood a very angry-looking elf.

"You thought you could trick me!" yelled Krickshap. "And now you will all pay!"

Sarah stood by the Ogg and Vesper, wondering if she could do anything to stop the fight she knew was coming. She feared many trolls and gnomes would be badly hurt.

From down the hall, a small bright light flew up the staircase and danced around the room, almost as if it was looking for something. All the gnomes and trolls stopped when they saw the flickering light, which flew right over to Sarah and danced in front of her eyes.

Sarah recognized the sprite right away. "Frieda!" she said. "I think you better get out of here right now!"

Frieda just laughed, then made a high-pitched whistle that Sarah could barely hear.

From down below, Sarah heard a muffled sound. It started as a low rumble that reminded Sarah of the sound of the underground subway trains in New York. The trolls and gnomes heard it too. They looked around trying to figure out what was making the noise. The rumbling quickly got louder and louder, and it soon sounded as loud as a train roaring past. It got so loud that everyone—gnomes, trolls, elf, and girl—had to put their hands over their ears.

"What is that?" yelled Krickshap as he looked uneasily around him. But no one could hear him.

From up the staircase came a swarm of sprites. There were so many that they almost appeared as one huge wall of light. It was their wings that were making the noise—so many sprites beating their wings together in flight.

"Goodness," said Vesper, yelling loudly so that he could be heard. "I never knew there were so many of them! There must be millions!"

The swarm flew into the hall, and the light they generated

was so bright that gnomes and trolls alike had to move their hands from their ears to shield their eyes. It was as if the very sun itself was in the room with them.

Thousands of sprites flew around Krickshap's head. He swatted at them and jabbed at them with his scepter.

The trolls, who hated the light even more than they hated the gnomes, moaned and grunted. They screamed and started running into each other. The army of gnomes blocked the only exit.

"Let's finish them off," yelled a gnome from the pack. "Once and for all!"

Vesper acted quickly. He ran to the side of the hall and pushed open another secret doorway.

He motioned to Sarah. "Get them to chase the trolls into here," he yelled, trying to be heard above the din.

Sarah looked up. She couldn't tell where Frieda was, but the sprites must have understood what Vesper said. They started herding the trolls toward the open door but they didn't need much convincing. The trolls ran from the room down into the dark passageway as fast as they could.

Krickshap screamed. "Come back! I order you!" He ran toward the trolls, poking several with the tip of his scepter. They yelled in pain, but did not stop.

The sprites guided all the terrified trolls down the passageway. When the last trolls and sprites had left, Vesper closed the secret door.

Then all was quiet.

Only one sprite had stayed, and she flew to Sarah's

shoulder. Frieda smiled.

The gnomes stood still. They didn't know what to do. The sound of the million beating wings had stopped, and the blinding light was gone.

Sarah and the Ogg ran to Vesper.

"Where does that go?" she asked.

"Outside," said Vesper with a smile. "Those trolls must be halfway to their caves by now."

Sarah looked at Vesper and kissed his cheek. Sarah thought his beard was very scratchy. Vesper just blushed.

The Ogg looked around. "Where is Krickshap?" he said. In all the confusion, no one had been able to see where he had gone.

"Maybe he got swept out in a sea of trolls," said Vesper.

The surprised army of gnomes lowered their swords. They gathered around Vesper.

"You let them escape," Mayfield Moontooth said to him. "They're the ones that took us from our homes. They turned us to stone!"

"That's right," murmured several gnomes in the crowd.

The Ogg raised his hand, and the crowd grew quiet. "It seems we may have been too hard on the trolls," he said. "They were acting out of fear of Krickshap."

"But we've never been able to get along with trolls," said Rumphus Borgalum. "Even before that elf showed up."

There was more murmuring from the crowd. Vesper thought of all the times he had chased the trolls from his land and all the troll traps he had seen. Then he thought of Ralph.

"Perhaps," said Vesper, "they simply don't like us because we were never nice to them."

A gnome made her way out of the crowd and put her arm around Vesper. It was Mazy.

"That may be the smartest thing you ever said," she laughed.

"Well, then," said the Ogg. "Maybe we should start getting everything back in order."

Sarah looked around the room. With all the commotion over, she decided to get a better look at the tapestries on the walls. One of them seemed to depict a familiar farmhouse. It was her house—or, rather, the Ogg's original home.

Vesper's mother came over and hugged him. "You were very brave," she said. "Maybe you should be a tracker like us now."

Vesper thought about that. "I'd like that," he said. "But I like to cook even more. I think I'll stay here in the mountain."

The quiet was broken by a sudden scream. The gnomes turned and looked at the front of the room. There stood Krickshap. In one bony hand he held his scepter, pointed at the neck of a prisoner he held tightly. It was Sarah.

CHAPTER 20

Gold

Krickshap had surprised Sarah when she had gone to the front to look at the tapestry. He had been hiding behind the Ogg's tall chair. Sarah tried to fight him, but his bony arms held her still.

All five hundred gnomes drew their swords and advanced toward the elf.

"Go ahead," said Krickshap with a sneer, "and I'll give the human here a jolt she will never recover from."

Vesper stood in front of the other gnomes. "He has us," he said, loudly enough that all could hear. "We'll have to give him what he wants most."

Krickshap's pointed ears perked up.

"What is that?" said a gnome in the back.

Vesper looked at the Ogg. "It's time to give him our gold."

"I knew it!" laughed Krickshap, still holding onto Sarah tightly. "I knew you stinking gnomes had gold! Now give it to me!"

There was a murmuring from the gnomes. The Ogg hushed them and looked at Vesper. He knew he was bluffing, because the gnomes really didn't have any gold, but he could not figure out what Vesper's plan was.

"Why don't you tell him where it is?" said the Ogg.

Vesper winked at him. He walked up to the very same tapestry Sarah had been looking at—the one showing the old farmhouse.

"No funny business," sneered Krickshap as he backed away from Vesper while still holding his prisoner.

Vesper looked at Sarah. "If you hurt her, there's no gold," he said defiantly.

Krickshap scowled. "Don't threaten me, you worm," he said. "Give me the gold NOW!" He held the scepter right up to Sarah's chin.

"Okay, okay," said Vesper. He turned to the huge tapestry hanging on the wall and grabbed the corner with both hands. He tugged hard, and the tapestry was ripped from the wall and fell to the stone floor below.

There, set in the wall, was what looked like an opening of some kind. It was all boarded up with crisscrossing planks of wood that seemed to be nailed right to the wall. All the gnomes gathered closer to see what it was.

"Get back, all of you!" yelled Krickshap. He pointed at the Ogg. "Get some of them to pry off the boards!"

The Ogg nodded to Mayfield Moontooth and his daughter Maya. It only took them a few whacks to chop the boards up.

With the boards gone, it was easy to see what they had been covering. There on the wall a doorway with a flowing leaf pattern intricately carved around the edges and a keyhole in the center.

Sarah immediately recognized it as a gnome-way. But hadn't Vesper told her that all the ones that opened with keys led to her world?

Krickshap laughed. "It's a treasure room!" he said. "Open it! Open it now!"

Vesper stepped forward. Around his neck, he still wore the chain with the key that the Ogg had given him. He removed the chain from his neck, put the key into the keyhole, and turned it. It made a loud click, and the door slowly opened. Vesper stepped back, closer to the Ogg.

Krickshap, still holding Sarah tightly, moved to the doorway and peered inside. It was totally dark, and he couldn't see a thing.

"The gold is inside," said the Ogg. "Go in and get it."

Krickshap thought about that for a moment. Then he turned to the Ogg.

"It's a trap," he said. He nodded to Vesper. "Send the cook in to grab some of the treasure and bring it to me!"

Vesper looked at the Ogg with a worried look on his face. He slowly walked to the doorway.

The Ogg walked in front of him. "I'll get it," he said.

Krickshap laughed as he pulled Sarah closer. "No!" he said. "Send in the little hero!"

That was all Sarah could take. She didn't know where the gnome-way led, but she knew it must not be good.

"Enough is enough!" she said, and what she did next was relived in song and retold in story to every gnome child at bedtime until the end of time.

In one continuous swoop, Sarah pulled her hand free, grabbed Krickshap's arm, and flipped him over her back. The eight-foot elf sailed in the air, dropped his scepter, and landed with a thud on the cold stone floor.

No one moved. Everyone was so surprised that they didn't know what to do.

"How did you know how to do that?" asked Vesper.

Sarah smiled. "Four years of karate," she said. "I'm surprised I didn't think of it earlier."

Krickshap quickly stood up. He looked for his scepter, but the Ogg had picked it up.

"Looking for this?" he said.

Now all the gnomes started to move toward Krickshap, their swords all rising into the air at once.

The elf knew he was trapped. He jumped and dove headfirst into the only exit he could reach—the gnome-way. The second his body made it all the way through, there was a loud WHOOSH sound, and he was gone.

Quickly, the Ogg shut the door and turned the key to lock it. It made a loud click. The Ogg pulled out the key and handed it back to Vesper.

Sarah ran over. "Where did he go?" she said. "I remember you saying all the gnome-ways with keys led to my world."

"They do," said Vesper. "But I wouldn't worry about him."

"Why not?" asked Sarah.

The Ogg smiled. "I told you that all the dangerous gnome-ways were boarded up," he said. "It was very clever of Vesper to remember this one behind the tapestry."

"Where does it go to?" asked Sarah. "Shouldn't we be worried?"

"Not unless elves are good at holding their breath," joked Vesper.

Sarah looked confused.

"A lot of gnomes lost their lives going through that gnome-way," said the Ogg. "That's why it was not only locked, but boarded up."

"But *where* does it go?" Sarah asked again.

"It opens in a very bad place," said the Ogg. "Right at the bottom of the Atlantic Ocean!"

CHAPTER 21

A Party

With Krickshap gone, the Ogg thought they all needed a party to celebrate. So, even though each gnome was anxious to get back to their own home, they all spent much of that day and the next happily cleaning and fixing up the mountain. The gnome woodcutters cut and stacked firewood for the fires. Sarah polished the silver and helped clean the kitchen, while Vesper rolled up his sleeves and cooked like he had never cooked before. The Ogg dug out his woodworking tools and repaired broken benches and tables. Even Mazy, who usually kept to herself, was laughing and telling stories as she helped sweep the great halls. Frieda and the other sprites danced above everyone's head while the gnomes worked.

There never was as grand and exciting a party as the one the gnomes threw that day. The musicians played their instruments while huge tables were set. Several gnomes danced and sang, while others were just happy to spend time with their families again. A troupe of gnome actors even put on a play about the adventures of Vesper and Sarah. Sarah thought it was very funny, even though the gnome who played her was very short. They even acted out the scene where Sarah threw the evil elf over her shoulder (the elf was played by a straw broom with a nasty face painted on it).

And then the food Vesper made was brought out. There were soups, salads, and fresh loaves of bread, along with five different main courses. There were so many desserts that, by the end of the meal, Sarah thought she would explode if she had one more bite. Sarah pushed herself from the table and got up. She walked around the great hall. The tapestry behind the Ogg's chair had been repaired and was again hanging proudly. She looked at the picture of the Ogg's farmhouse—her farmhouse. She thought of her parents and how worried they must be.

While she was staring at the tapestry, she felt a hand on her shoulder. Sarah looked up and saw the Ogg standing next to her, also looking at the tapestry. In his hand, he was holding the photograph of himself and Lavenia.

"It's a beautiful house," he said. "And I think it's time you got back there."

Sarah smiled and hugged him.

After the feast, Vesper clanked his mug lightly with his sword to get everyone's attention. All the gnomes stopped their talking and were quiet. Vesper stood up.

"I want to make a toast to the person we have to thank for our rescue. Without her, all of us would still be collecting dust." The crowd laughed.

Vesper raised his mug. "A toast to Sarah, the elf-thrower. May the moon and the stars always guide her safely."

All the gnomes clinked their mugs. "To Sarah!"

Sarah got up and stood on her chair. "I want to make a toast too!" she said, raising her mug. "To my friend Vesper, who is not only brave, but also a wonderful friend!"

"To Vesper!" the gnomes cheered. Vesper's father slapped him on his back. "That's my son," he said.

The Ogg had been quietly sitting in his tall chair at the front of one of the main tables. He cheered at the toasts and laughed along with the stories, but his mind kept wandering. He kept getting up and looking at the tapestry behind him, staring at the image of his home in the upper world.

All the gnomes were tired. Most would leave the mountain the next day to go to their huts and homes. They were anxious to get back to their everyday lives. Just before everyone went off to find a room or a cozy corner to sleep in, the Ogg rose from his chair.

There was an instant hush from the crowd. "The Ogg is going to speak," they muttered, as they forgot their drowsiness and sat straight in their seats.

"I want to thank all of you for your bravery and courage," he said. "We gnomes have always stood together in good times and bad. We have always been one family."

There were shouts and cheers from the crowd. "Cheers to the Ogg. Cheers to the One Great Gnome!" they called. The Ogg smiled, but waved his hands to quiet them down.

"When I came here long ago," he continued, "you took me in and made me one of you. You are my family now. So it will be very hard for me to say goodbye."

CHAPTER 22

A Journey Home

"What do you mean?" the gnomes shouted.

Vesper ran to the Ogg's side. "Where are you going?" he asked.

The Ogg smiled and pointed at the tapestry. "I'm not getting any younger," he said. "And I want to see my old farmhouse again. If Sarah will let me go with her, I think I'll go for a visit. So don't think of it as a goodbye—just think of it as a vacation. I promise to come back."

Sarah stood next to the Ogg. "It's your house," she said. "We can find some other place to live."

"No, no," laughed the Ogg. "That house is yours and your family's," he said. "But do you think they would mind a guest for a bit? Maybe I could help get the old house back into shape."

Sarah thought of the house and the rough shape it was in. Then she thought of her father and his hurt thumbs.

"I think they would love to have you," she said. "I would too."

"But what about us?" asked Vesper. "We need you here. Who will help us rebuild our homes or help us plan our future? We need the Ogg to show us!"

The Ogg thought about this.

"I think you're right," he told Vesper. "Everyone," he shouted, "while I am gone, I hereby declare that Vesper of Oglinoth—who has shown his great bravery and friendship—will become the next Ogg!"

There were murmurs from the crowd.

"I can't be the Ogg!" sputtered Vesper. "I have… I have… cooking to do!"

"Then you will be the Ogg who cooks, but who can still help things run smoothly around here," said the Ogg.

Sarah hugged Vesper. "Hurray for Vesper, the new Ogg!" she shouted.

The gnomes all stood and bowed to Vesper. "Long live the Ogg!" they shouted.

"Both of them!" laughed Mazy from the back of the room.

The next day, most of the gnomes left the mountain to go back to their homes. Sarah and the Ogg headed back to the gnome-way by Mazy's house. Vesper insisted on walking them all the way.

"Isn't there a gnome-way around here?" Sarah asked.

"Well, I think there's one by that tree," said the Ogg, smiling. "But that one takes us to India, and that's too long of a walk home for me."

The Ogg was traveling with a bag slung over his back, filled with his tools. "It sounds like I'll need these," he said. Some gnomes had volunteered to carry the pack for him all the way to the gnome-way, but the Ogg just sent them away, saying, "I'm not that old!"

Sarah had thought Mazy would join them on the walk home, seeing as her house was on the way. But Mazy had loved the company so much in the mountain that she'd decided to give up living alone and stay. She'd even offered to give Vesper some cooking lessons when he got back. He was not happy about that.

Frieda and several sprites did join the group on the trip. They danced in front of them and kept their path well-lit.

When they passed the Statue of Liberty, the Ogg had to stop. He looked up at the carving of his wife. "I'm going home, Lavenia," he said. "I want to make sure your gardens are alive and well."

In late afternoon they stopped to rest by a stream, and Sarah thought she saw a shadow move between some trees in the distance. She couldn't be sure, but it seemed like the shape of a troll.

"I hope Ralph will be fine," she said.

Vesper looked at Sarah. "I'll find him," he said, "and make sure he is." Then Vesper turned to the Ogg. "And one of my first responsibilities will be to help the trolls. Just like you helped us."

The Ogg just smiled.

After a long day's walk, they made it to Vesper's parents' home. His parents had arrived earlier in the day. They all helped clean the place. Vesper made dinner for everyone, but the Ogg insisted that Vesper sit in the tall chair that his father had carved. When Vesper refused, they finally agreed that Sarah should rightly be the one. Sarah was embarrassed, but thought the chair was still very comfy.

They all headed to bed early. It had been a long day. "No need for cream-of-beetroot soup tonight," yawned Vesper as they all settled in for the night.

Sarah scrunched up in the tiny bed again, hoping that at this time tomorrow she would be in her own bed. She missed her parents and hoped she had not worried them too much.

As Sarah was trying to drift off to sleep, she saw Frieda fly in through the window and land on the pillow next to her head. She smiled at Sarah and kissed her on the cheek.

"Thanks for your help and friendship," Sarah whispered to the sprite. "I'll miss you very much."

Frieda understood. She smiled again and waved once, then flew out the window into the night.

After a simple breakfast the next day, the friends were off. Vesper's parents made a big fuss over Sarah and told her she could come stay with them any time. As they left, Vesper's parents hugged him. "Our son, the Ogg," they said.

Soon they had finally arrived at the old tree behind the field at Mazy's house. The gnome-way was, of course, still there. Its shiny keyhole glistened in the sun. Vesper and Sarah were quiet. They knew the time had come for them to say goodbye, but the words didn't come easily.

The Ogg wanted to give them some time alone. "I see some Dragon's Breath," he said. "Maybe I'll pick some to take back with me." And he strode off into the field.

The two friends stood in silence.

"I'd still be a hunk of stone if it wasn't for you," Vesper finally said.

"And you were a friend when I needed one the most," said Sarah.

Vesper rummaged inside his backpack and pulled something out. It was a small sword. It looked a lot like his, except there was a carving of a little farmhouse on the handle.

"Every gnome has to have a sword," he said, handing it to her. "And from this time forth, you are not only a human, but you are a gnome, too."

Sarah took the sword and kissed his cheek again. It was still very scratchy, but she didn't care. Then she and Vesper hugged tightly—the kind of hug that you never want to end.

The Ogg came back and pulled a chain out from his vest pocket. It had a key on the end of it.

Vesper felt around his neck. His key was still there.

"I had another one made," said the Ogg. "This way, we can both come back and forth anytime we want."

"I'd like that," said Vesper.

The Ogg put the key into the lock and turned it. The door opened with a loud click. He took the key out and put it safely into his vest.

Vesper and the Ogg hugged, then Vesper started to walk away. But he stopped and turned toward his friends.

"May the moon and the stars always guide you safely… back to me."

Then Vesper turned and ran off.

The Ogg looked into the hole, and then he looked at his belly. "May be a tight fit, but I think I'll make it," he said.

"I'll go first," said Sarah, and she bent down to crawl into the hole.

"Wait one second," said the Ogg. "I have to warn you of something."

"What?" asked Sarah.

The Ogg kneeled on the ground by the tree. "I'm afraid time does not run the same in the upper world as it does here," he said.

Sarah was confused. "What do you mean?"

"I remember," said the Ogg, "when I first came here, I had forgotten some tools, so I took the gnome-way home. I wasn't gone more than a half hour when I came back out right here."

"Yes," said Sarah. "And what happened?"

"The gnomes asked why I had been gone so long," he continued. "To them I had been gone for a month."

"So time moves more quickly here?" Sarah asked, not sure what that would mean.

"Not always," said the Ogg. "Once, I went home for some books, and I actually got back a day before I left!"

"So what does that mean?" asked Sarah.

"It means I don't know how much time will have gone by when you get home," said the Ogg. "That's one of the reasons I had decided to stay here full-time."

Sarah didn't know what to think.

"You mean… I could go back, and maybe months have gone by?" she said.

"Or years," said the Ogg.

"Well, there is only one way to find out," said Sarah as she turned and crawled into the opening. As soon as her feet were inside, she heard the loud WHOOSH sound and felt herself falling up into darkness.

CHAPTER 23

Stories End

Sarah was tumbling. She couldn't see or hear anything. She tried to look below her to see if the Ogg was behind her, but she could only see blackness.

Then, up above her head, she saw a shaft of light, and then she popped out of the tunnel and landed with a thud on a dirt floor. Sarah looked around her. It was the potting shed. It was still a wreck, and she was lucky not to have landed on any of the broken glass.

She stood up. It was daylight. She wondered how long she had been gone. Just then, she heard a WHOOSH and saw a bag filled with tools shoot out of the gnome-way and land in a heap in the corner. She had just enough time to move out of the way before the Ogg himself flew up through the opening and landed on his back by her feet.

"Ouch," he said. "I forgot how much that can hurt."

Sarah helped him to his feet and dusted the dirt from his jacket. The Ogg stared all around him, and his mouth fell open.

"Oh my! I didn't know it had gotten this bad," he said. "Is the rest of the house like this?"

Before Sarah could answer, she heard her name being called.

"Sarah," called the voice. "Sarah, where are you?"

It was her father. Sarah left the Ogg and ran out of the potting shed, following the voice to the front of the house. As she turned the corner, she saw her father, holding a paper bag and looking at his watch.

"Dad!" called Sarah. "I'm here!"

She ran up to her father and almost tackled him to the ground with a bear hug.

"Easy! Easy, kiddo," said her father, lifting the bag up over his head. "You'll squish your mother's lunch."

"Mom's lunch?" said Sarah.

"Did you forget already?" her father said. "It's Mom's first day at work, and I thought we would surprise her by bringing her favorite lunch. It's liverwurst on rye."

Sarah couldn't believe it. "How long have I been gone?" she asked.

"Gone?" her father said. "Gone where? You just ran by here a few minutes ago."

Sarah hugged her dad once more. "It's so nice to see you again!"

Just then, Sarah's father noticed a man walking toward them—a large man with a long, full white beard, looking at the house and shaking his head. He seemed to be carrying a heavy bag of tools. Sarah saw him too.

She ran over and brought the man to her father.

"Dad, this is a friend I… just met. His name is the Ogg—I mean, Otis Grimwald!"

Her father shook the man's hand. Although he had just met him, Sarah's father could tell he was a kind man. He noticed that the man kept looking at the condition of the house.

"Nice to meet you, Otis," Sarah's father said. "We just moved in, and I know the place needs some repairs. Well… a lot of repairs."

"Can I help?" asked Otis. "I've been known to be pretty handy with tools." He winked at Sarah.

Sarah's father looked at his still-bandaged thumb. "Otis, I

would LOVE some help," he said. "I'd like to bring this place back to what it looked like when it was new."

"I think that's a grand idea!" said Otis. "But I'm going to need lots of supplies. Wood, nails, new shingles for the roof…"

"Okay, okay," laughed Sarah's father. "You make the list while Sarah and I bring her mom her lunch. Then we'll get to work!"

Sarah and her father left Otis. He was busy making a long list of supplies, but Sarah saw a big grin on his face as they drove onto the road.

"It's funny," her father said as they drove along, "but Mr. Grimwald looks a bit like that statue you found."

"Yes," said Sarah smiling. "Just like one great gnome."

The End

Author's Note

I started writing this book when my sons were young. They were fans of stories like *The Lord of the Rings*, but I wanted to find something that was aimed at a younger audience. So I decided to write my own.

It's easy to see my influences. This book has echoes from my favorite stories, from *The Wizard of Oz* to *Alice in Wonderland*. I have always loved tales about kids in magical worlds.

I also wanted to acknowledge another influence. I have always been a fan of the book *The Cricket in Times Square,* by George Selden. The original had many sequels, but my favorite was called *Tucker's Countryside.* In that book, Harry Cat and Tucker Mouse leave the comforts of their home in New York City and venture out to the fictional town of Hadley, Connecticut. I had moved from the Bronx to Connecticut when I was 11 years old, so that book resonated with me. That's why I chose to have Sarah move to the same town in this book.

I hope you enjoyed the story, and remember what Vesper says:

May the moon and the stars always guide you safely.

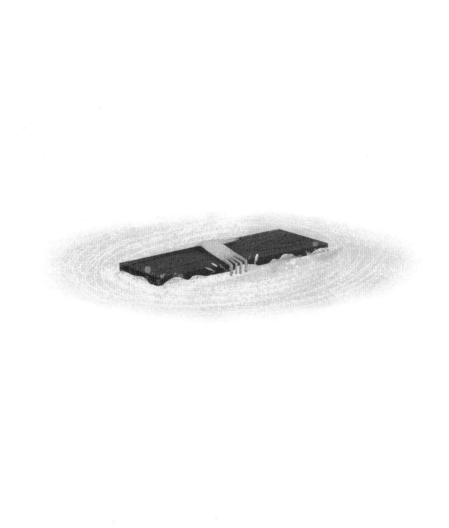